The author served in the British Army during the Cold War after reading modern languages at Jesus College, Oxford. Over the course of his career he spent a good deal of time gathering military intelligence in communist eastern Europe. This included three years as a ground operations officer with the British Commander-in-Chief's Mission to the Soviet Forces in (East) Germany, and four years as a military attaché at the British Embassy in Warsaw. He is now retired and lives with his wife in Wiltshire.

With very best wishes to my good friends, Jenny and Steve, ~ fellow conservationists, also familiar with sound of the guns on Larkhill.

Jeremy H

UNEASY
Sleepers

J H Jorvik

SilverWood

Published in 2017 by SilverWood Books

SilverWood Books Ltd
14 Small Street, Bristol, BS1 1DE, United Kingdom
www.silverwoodbooks.co.uk

ISBN 978-1-78132-551-3 (paperback)
ISBN 978-1-78132-552-0 (ebook)

British Library Cataloguing in Publication Data
A CIP catalogue record for this book is available from
the British Library

Page design and typesetting by SilverWood Books
Printed on responsibly sourced paper

Remembering Maria Matlak, who arrived in Auschwitz-Birkenau
alone, aged fifteen, on 2nd April 1943

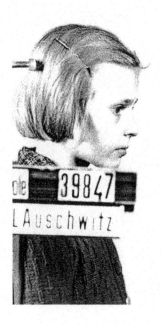

I

'*Paskudny chłopaku!*'

Stefan, aged four, was used to being good-humouredly addressed as a "wretched boy". This mild rebuke came from the only person in his uncertain world to whom he could look for security and protection. The girl seemed to be constantly hurrying him along, tugging him by the cuff of his sleeve, hardly ever holding him by the hand.

Zamość was not a good place to be in November 1942. Poland was enduring its third year of Nazi occupation, and mass deportations were in progress to give Germans the *Lebensraum* (living space) their Führer craved. Little Stefan understood none of this, but he knew that Zamość was now a bad place to be in because the girl had told him so.

The two spindly figures running along the railway station platform drew little attention to themselves; they were swept along by jostling crowds searching for seats or standing room on the train which was about to depart for Lublin. The girl had a compact canvas rucksack slung on her back and was carrying a small, cheap fabric suitcase; in her other hand she was clutching the all-important papers supplied to her by the recently established underground organisation Żegota, which would allow her, and her small charge, to travel far away from this newly proclaimed German enclave. The boy carried only a light satchel containing woollen gloves, a few washing things, some chunks of bitter chocolate and a familiar threadbare soft toy; also a miniature Roman Catholic missal which he was unlikely to read, even when old enough to do so.

They finally reached the front end of the train, anxious and out of breath. Stefan was momentarily riveted by the huge black steam locomotive with its heavy wheels, shining pistons and large rectangular smoke deflectors. But he quickly took cover behind the girl when a jet of superheated steam and a deafening whistle exploded simultaneously from the straining monster. She pushed him roughly up and ahead of her through the only open door in the leading carriage. She then flung herself, along with her rucksack and suitcase, into the corridor as the solid carriage door was slammed heavily behind her. She grimaced at her bony, bruised knees.

After so much exertion and excitement there was now an even higher priority than finding two seats. Stefan found himself closeted with the girl in a dingy on-board WC. This unavoidable ritual had become something of a crisis which he disliked more and more each time, as it involved much over-supervision, haste and anxiety; here, in brief privacy, the girl could not disguise her disapproval of the small boy's irrevocable secret which, if revealed to a German or even to some of her fellow countrymen, could land them both behind barbed wire.

Once they were back in the corridor they set about finding

somewhere to sit. An elderly couple hastily stacked their hand baggage on the rack above their heads and squeezed together to make room for the young pair to sit.

'So are you two travelling far?'

The girl looked directly at the old woman, sizing her up before replying.

'I am caring for this child while we move to another area.' The almost unendurable responsibility that had been thrust upon her over the past few weeks had given her an air of gravitas and maturity, and mistrust, well beyond her fourteen years.

After a few kilometres of clanking and lurching out of Zamość and into the bleak, snow-clad countryside, a railway official, accompanied by a German soldier, came into the carriage compartment. He glanced fleetingly at Stefan and the girl, and after a perfunctory examination of their papers quickly handed them back. He went on to give those of the other passengers noticeably closer scrutiny, dutifully passing them to the Wehrmacht corporal for inspection. He had no doubt guessed that the two children were soon to be spirited out of Poland, and he must have silently wished them well.

The train journey continued uneventfully for several hours before a change of scenery, and general air of anticipation, heralded their arrival in Lublin. Here the two children had to change trains for their onward journey. There was a pleasant enough atmosphere of normality, with very few German troops in evidence. The girl nodded unsmilingly as the kindly old couple bade her farewell. She hurried with the small boy to a ticket office window where she enquired about the next train bound for Warsaw. She then purchased some rye bread and sausage from a stall, snatching them away from Stefan as he eagerly reached for them; these were to be eaten later. A small group of people, including children, were singing and joking around an elderly accordionist playing popular tunes in return for small change further along the platform. The girl was not tempted to join in. She was probably thinking of the now infamous Majdanek concentration camp only some five kilometres away. Stefan, however, was feeling cheerful and looked up at the girl expectantly, searching for a smile. None was forthcoming.

A rapid announcement came over the station loudspeaker, and a long train, hauled by another gigantic steam locomotive, slowly screeched to a halt at the platform on which Stefan and the girl were standing anxiously. They clambered aboard and quickly found two seats. The train accelerated rapidly. After a few minutes the girl asked a lady in black to keep their seats for them, and dragged a reluctant Stefan off to the WC at the end of the corridor. This time it was she who needed to use it first. Stefan watched, unembarrassed, as she went about her business, and was impressed to see a stash of paper money protruding from a pocket sewn inside her grey cotton knickers. She signalled to him, against the roar of the lurching train, to say nothing of what he had seen. The little boy nodded enthusiastically; he felt privileged to be a party to this important secret.

Once back in the carriage compartment Stefan settled back into a state of sullen boredom. He was feeling tired, and was no longer interested in the passing snowbound scenery outside. Instead he let his gaze fall on his girl guardian, who was staring out through the carriage window and into the distance. Her demeanour was reassuringly familiar to him. Her brown hair, cut straight above the nape of her neck and pinned back with a small sprung hairgrip, framed a thin face with deep-set dark eyes and a distinctive mouth. She had a very slightly protruding lower lip which looked somewhat severe in repose and only rarely broke into a pursed, wry smile. Stefan both respected and quite liked her when she would lower her head, look him straight in the eye and dryly reprove him from time to time. To him she was strong and capable.

After a while the girl unwrapped the rye bread and sausage from their newspaper and shared them with Stefan. Then both slept fitfully through a night of frequent halts along the main line to Warsaw. Long trains carrying German heavy military equipment invariably took priority over all other rail traffic at that time.

It was just before dawn when the train finally pulled into Warsaw Central Station. Stefan awoke sulkily to find himself being shaken by the arm and told to put on his woollen gloves and to sling his satchel on his back. He and the girl then hurried along the corridor. They jumped down on to a platform teeming with soldiers in field grey uniform. The boy was suddenly wide awake and taking note of everything around him. Papers were checked again at the platform barrier.

This time a German civilian official looked suspiciously at the two children and asked, 'Where are your parents?'

The girl replied promptly, in halting German, 'I have not seen them since we left Zamość.'

Their papers were handed back to her, and both children were waved impatiently through the barrier.

Once out of the station and on Aleje Jerozolimskie, the girl stood still for a moment, frowning at a city which she could scarcely have recognised since her last visit, with her heavily pregnant mother, in the summer of 1941. The sun had been beating down then, imbuing heaps of bomb rubble with a life of their own; flowering weeds had shot up between shattered masonry, and street trading among the ruins had been optimistic and brisk. She had already told Stefan about the wooden handcarts full of small tortoises, an odd consequence of the German invasion of Greece. Her mother, a hard-working and clandestine schoolteacher, had reluctantly purchased one of these for her, a small reward for her perseverance with English. The child had designated it her loyal companion in anticipation of another ecliptic sibling, and had named it, appropriately, Tomasz. The animal had recently subsided into its third or fourth hibernation. Now the girl shivered as she gazed on streets still extensively in ruins but covered in ice and snow, streets whose inhabitants were resigned to an unending occupation by conquerors who bore them only ill will.

II

The sky was just beginning to lighten as Stefan and the girl started walking down Aleje Ujazdowskie. They were moving away from the city centre and in the opposite direction to the urban ghetto from where thirty-two thousand Jewish townspeople had already been transported to an extermination camp near an insignificant little village called Treblinka. Warsaw was by now under threat of destruction, in every respect and at every level. The two children, however, did not really sense this as they passed defiant symbols and slogans daubed on walls. They saw flowers and guttering candles at spots where summary executions had taken place, and small groups of boy and girl scouts energetically clearing rubble or carrying out mundane errands on behalf of those working secretly for the survival of the city's population. At one point the girl glanced up and spotted three young boys hanging around on a rooftop. She would have guessed that these were *Zawiszacy*, organised to watch and report on low-level German activity on the streets below.

Just as they reached the north end of Belwederska two men waved them across to the opposite side of the road so that they would not pass too close to some corpses lying with only their legs showing from beneath blankets. The four had been executed just minutes earlier, hence no candles or flowers. The girl looked across at two old women sobbing woefully nearby, and noticed blood trickling from the blanketed bodies.

Stefan asked why they were lying there.

Her curt reply, '*Śpią*' – "they're asleep" – was enough to satisfy his curiosity, and she resolved to hurry him on, but where to now?

The girl had instructions to rendezvous at a safe house in the suburbs, but not before last light; so she began to outline to Stefan a plan which she had already worked out. They would spend the rest of the day having a good time in Łazienki Park. There were woods and valleys, lakes and bridges, a palace and pavilions where they could wander, keep out of the cold and have something to eat, and she would give Stefan his first lesson in English.

Stefan spent much of the next seven hours shuffling through the snow. He happily coaxed winsome red squirrels which mingled fearlessly with the few strollers while foraging for acorns and fir cones. He chased ducks at the frozen water's edge, and ran breathlessly up and down challenging slopes. The girl remained darkly watchful, keeping a close eye on the small boy, while constantly observing the movements of any stranger who might purposefully approach them. Her thoughts would have been on shelter and food to enable them to cope with the encroaching cold, and she would have begun to worry when it became clear that most of the buildings in the park had either been gutted by fire or were closed for the winter.

So she was quick to shepherd Stefan into a drab but well-heated tea room which they eventually came upon at one end of the partly derelict orangery. There was little food to be had there, but they were given a small cast-iron table and two chairs to themselves and made do with weak beetroot soup and one chunk of black bread between them. After a while an incongruously trim waitress appeared. She smiled at them, and told them they could sit there for as long as they liked. A few moments later she reappeared with a small packet. This contained dry biscuits and had only a serial number on its wrapping. She said the biscuits were issued to British soldiers. Stefan was curious but, after quizzing the young waitress, he was none the wiser. He eagerly slipped the packet into his satchel. The girl forestalled any further questions by digging out from the bottom of her rucksack one of two immeasurably precious objects; this was a Polish-English elementary grammar book which had been scribbled on and well thumbed by her mother's latent pupils back in Zamość.

Choosing her words carefully, she managed to impress on Stefan that learning English was the single most important thing he would be doing from now on. As she began to read aloud strange-sounding words from the opening pages, encouraging Stefan to repeat after her, he became totally absorbed. She went on to read out whole sentences. He did not understand these, but every cadence, every tonal inflexion enchanted the little boy. And so in the isolation of that small refuge both children were fleetingly wafted away from the war on a gentle and iridescent stream of language which somehow linked them to other people; to another world. And for the first time Stefan felt a momentary and comfortable kinship with his slender and solitary guardian.

Suddenly the girl noticed the time on a wall clock above their table. She repacked her rucksack with care and called out thanks to the waitress who had disappeared into the adjoining kitchen. Then she hastily pushed Stefan ahead of her through the door and out into the cold evening air.

They made their way through the park and back to Belwederska. As they trudged further towards the southern outskirts of the city, and into Mokotów district, a biting wind began to lash their faces from across the River Vistula. The girl pulled a canvas and wool peaked cap over Stefan's head and offered to carry his satchel, but he would not be parted from it.

After another half-hour's walk they came to a small rubble-blocked cul-de-sac signed "Podbipięty". As the girl sang out the name of the street Stefan knew that they were very soon to be among friends. The grey flat-roofed house, which they reached through a tall iron gate, was much bigger than he had expected. Even as they were climbing stone steps towards the front door it was quickly opened. An elderly round-faced man with thinning grey hair ushered them in and quietly closed the door behind them. He greeted the girl gently, politely kissing her hand, notwithstanding her tender years; this was in deference, perhaps, to her demanding role in loco parentis. Stefan, by contrast, received a friendly arm around his shoulders. Their modest baggage was deposited in the lofty galleried hall, and they were gratefully led to two wooden chairs set before a tall ceramic stove. The intense heat which it radiated warmed their damp clothes and frozen faces, and visibly raised their spirits. The girl's eyes lit up on the appearance of two large bowls of thick potato soup. But even before she could take her first spoonful Stefan was slurping noisily, burning his tongue in the process. She looked at him, lowered her chin a little and scolded him, but with an unsuccessfully suppressed smile which made him laugh out loud. No sooner had they both finished their soup than Stefan saw that the girl's eyelids were flickering and her head nodding. He was struck by this first lapse of vigilance in at least ten days.

They rounded off supper with bottled plums, and then their courteous host, Pan Ludwik Rakowski, led the two children upstairs and showed them into separate rooms where their things had already been carried up from the hall. The girl must have felt momentary concern at the prospect of her young charge sleeping alone. But she showed rather more alarm at finding her rucksack next to a warm stove. Pan Rakowski graciously complied with her request to have it taken down to the cool cellar. He explained that his wife, Pani Jadwiga, was in poor health, but that they would be meeting her in the morning. He bade the children goodnight. Within minutes both had sunk into a dreamless sleep in the warmth of their respective rooms.

It was still dark outside when Stefan was awoken by the girl. She was already dressed and was struggling with a large jug of hot water. She filled the washbasin in his room, and told him to get up and wash his face and then to go downstairs without delay. Soon the two children were seated with Pan Rakowski and his wife around a sturdy table devouring a wholesome breakfast of freshly baked bread and a hard-boiled egg divided equally between them. After a while Pan Rakowski announced that two important people would be arriving very shortly. Neither the girl nor Stefan were to ask them who they were, but should pay close attention to all that they would be told. Their very lives could depend on it. Stefan watched the girl as she listened impassively.

Ten minutes later there was a muffled knock on the side door of the house, and two young men were let in without ceremony. They were clearly well known to the Rakowskis. Ignoring Stefan, they sat down at the table on either side of the girl and spread out the contents of a creased brown envelope which they had brought with them. While Pan Rakowski looked on in silence the girl was briefed by each man in turn and handed various skilfully forged documents. These, God willing, would provide safe passage out of occupied Poland and thence by sea to Sweden and finally to England. The two men must have realised that they were dealing with an exceptionally resourceful and resilient fourteen-year-old. They gave her a list of key contacts whose singular fitness for their role lay in the fact that there was nothing to link them, save only a brave resolve to help anyone attempting to escape Nazi persecution. Glancing across at Pan Rakowski, they concluded by warning the girl not to expect a rapturous welcome in England. A good number of British people now blamed their war on the Poles, and there were others in high places who valued the friendship of the Soviet Union above that of Poland.

Throughout the briefing she had been listening intently to every word, and nodding quietly. Now she had just one question for her interlocutors.

'When shall I return to Poland?'

There was a palpable silence; then one of the men touched her lightly on the arm, laughed pleasantly and said, 'Don't you worry yourself about that now – there's a great deal you have to do in the meantime. We wish you and the little boy the best of luck. Perhaps we shall see you again some day.'

They departed as suddenly as they had arrived. Pan Rakowski sat down beside the girl and went over one or two points of detail to make sure that she had fully understood them.

The rest of the day passed quickly. No time was wasted. The two children were checked carefully for any items which might arouse the suspicions of German police, soldiers or the Gestapo. Pan Rakowski went carefully through the contents of the girl's suitcase; then delved into the rucksack. He found nothing to cause concern, but just as he was about to help her repack it he peered again into the bottom of the bag, and espied something that made him raise his eyebrows. He made no comment, and together they carefully put everything back. There was now no question of cramming in the extra clothes and food which had been assembled for the journey; space for these was duly found in the compact fabric suitcase and in the boy's satchel. Finally Pani Jadwiga handed the girl a small, inexpensive watch. Her husband was surprised at the number of additional holes which he had to drill in the narrow leather strap before it would fit the girl's fragile wrist.

After a couple of telephone calls had been made, and the children's papers checked over for the last time, they all sat down to an early lunch. Soon afterwards a small car drew up outside the house. Pan Ludwik forced a smile and Pani Jadwiga cried a little as the car departed, with the two children, for Praga railway station on the east bank of the Vistula.

III

The train journey north to Gdynia, glibly renamed Gotenhafen by the invaders, should have been straightforward. As it happened, a German ammunition train had been derailed by the Home Army, the AK, much further along the line just south of Danzig. Consequently, by late that evening Stefan and the girl had got no further than Malbork. Here they had to leave the train without any prospect of continuing by rail for at least twenty-four hours. The girl must have taken heart from the thought that they were now less than fifty kilometres from the coast, but there was an immediate problem: her secret list of contacts did not include anyone in this small town on the banks of the River Nogat. There was a certain irony in this unscheduled stop-off. The town was still dominated by a massive brick citadel built by the Teutonic Knights as part of their thirteenth-century chain of defences along the Baltic seaboard.

As the two children were leaving the station there was a sudden fracas. A small group of Jewish rail travellers wearing the mandatory yellow Star of David were set upon by a snarling Alsatian under the control of its German police dog handler. While the animal snapped viciously at exposed hands and legs, two other German policemen moved in with flailing truncheons to finally subdue the bewildered men and women. At the same moment a large black van with barred windows arrived to take them away. But just as the dog was being pulled off the luckless victims by its handler it turned and bit Stefan on the leg. He screamed and clung, terrified, to the girl. She quickly drew him away, bruised and bleeding, to a quieter corner of the station entrance hall. As she began tending his injuries, urging him all the while to calm down, one of the Jews, a young man who had somehow escaped arrest in the earlier mêlée, came over and offered to help. The girl shook her head and waved him away.

Stefan had almost recovered his composure when a young girl aged about sixteen, wearing overalls and with her fair hair in plaits, and who had witnessed the incident, came up and said, 'That little boy needs medical attention. Come with me.'

She led them out of the station and along unlit streets to a single-storey wooden house next to a small workshop of some kind. Justyna – she had introduced herself by then – invited the two children into a warm and comfortable room where her mother set about dabbing and bandaging Stefan's wounds. These, she assured them, were not serious and would soon heal. In the course of the evening it transpired that Justyna's mother was a volunteer nurse on call to the AK. Like so many women of her generation she was a dedicated patriot, and was now keenly interested in the incipient exploits of Stefan and the girl. The sabotage of the ammunition train between Malbork and Danzig seemed to come as no surprise to her. She explained that her husband was away, but that she had a younger brother living nearby who would be happy to drive them in his lorry to their destination in Gdynia the next day. After a filling meal – food was generally easier to come by in the provinces – Justyna gave up her cramped bedroom to the two children. They fell asleep at once.

It was four o'clock in the morning when Stefan and the girl were awoken by urgent voices outside their room. Justyna came in with a flickering lantern, and told them to get up and dress, and to be ready to leave as soon as possible. Her uncle, Pan Antoni, would have to get them to Gdynia and be back in Malbork himself before dawn. He was a sturdily built and genial man who sported a bushy dark moustache in the style of Piłsudski. He was also a thoroughly proficient mechanic and had been persuaded by his sister to make his expertise available to the AK.

Once the two children were aboard the small lorry, with their light baggage, he checked that they had their papers to hand, and they drove off into the darkness. Although Pan Antoni chatted cheerfully to the children as he negotiated a series of minor roads, little Stefan was soon fast asleep against the girl's shoulder.

Over the next ten days Stefan lost all track of time and space as he and the girl were swept along by fast-moving and, to him, largely unfathomable events. To start with, endless hours seemed to be spent waiting around in houses and offices while people came and went, perusing papers and speaking quietly and intently with the girl. All the complexities involved passed entirely over his head: validation of documents, shipping agents' procedures, international law governing Swedish neutrality and current German policy on the expatriation of children registered as non-Jewish. He coped with this flood of unfamiliarity by anchoring himself to what he knew and understood. For the first time in weeks he clutched his threadbare toy, a drab flannel and wool rat-like animal. It had no name but afforded a welcome link with those friendlier strangers who took a moment to have a passing word with the small boy.

Finally they went to sea. In between periods of being wretchedly seasick in the bowels of a pitching and yawing Swedish timber freighter he would ask the girl to teach him more English. Conditions at sea allowed only occasional, and very brief, daylight excursions on deck. During these Stefan gazed on towering grey walls of water with awe and alarm. This first exposure to the menacing and impersonal force of nature was for him the stuff of nightmares. Even his premature experience of war bore no comparison. Both he and the girl had somehow come to terms with all that.

And so Stefan was happy when the ship eventually anchored off Helsingborg on the west coast of Sweden. A suspected drifting sea mine delayed the vessel's docking for almost four hours. The two children were then taken ashore and into a brightly lit built-up area which clearly had neither experience nor expectation of night bombing.

The next three days were spent in various comfortably furnished offices. Meetings between the girl and uniformed officials were punctuated by generous meals and two long nights beneath warm eiderdowns. Neither of the children could settle down to unbroken sleep. And so, with no need for a blackout against enemy air attack, the girl spent the odd hour with the light on giving Stefan more language tuition. So intrigued was he by the lavish English use of the personal pronoun (rarely coupled with verbs in Polish) that whenever he spoke the word "I" or "you" he would point with satisfaction at himself or at the girl. Simple dialogue was soon flowing between them. Conscious of the new life that lay ahead of the boy, she struck an intelligent balance between essential phrases and basic grammar. Thus they found restorative sleep between maelstroms of syntax, vocabulary and eccentric English idiom.

The next leg of their journey was short but pivotal: a five-kilometre choppy night crossing in a small motor boat from the bright lights of Helsingborg to the pitch darkness of Helsingør in German-occupied Denmark. No sooner had they set foot on the quay there, than they were hastily escorted on foot to a mooring some twenty minutes away and secure from infrequent German surveillance along that section of the Danish coastline. By now the wind had got up, and a heavy sea swell was breaking on the shore. Stefan shivered as he, the girl and their burly escort waited in the darkness while all kinds of heavy equipment were manhandled along a small gangplank and on to a wooden jetty. He could discern nothing beyond the muffled hubbub of all this Stygian and frenzied activity.

Quite soon all that remained at the jetty was the briefly lingering smell of oxyacetylene equipment. The two children were quickly pushed along the gangplank, and then strong hands lowered them through a small steel hatch. By now Stefan was familiar with the metallic sounds and oily aroma which meant another sea voyage. He felt disappointed at the prospect of yet more discomfort and seasickness. He and the girl were guided along a poorly lit passageway, cluttered with steel gadgetry, to a confined space where there was just enough improvised bedding for the two of them. They sat rigid and still in the peculiar dim red light while members of the crew swung into action. Brisk orders were given and diesel engines started running. Stefan prodded the girl excitedly.

'They're speaking English, aren't they?'

She nodded. Within a few minutes a slight rolling motion indicated that they were at sea, but soon after that there was no movement to speak of. Remembering the strong wind and the waves which had earlier been battering the shore, Stefan was puzzled, and relieved, that they were aboard a vessel that was so stable. Once the crew had settled down to their various routine tasks, one of them, a swarthy bearded matelot wearing sea boots and with his crushed peaked cap at a jaunty angle, came to where the two children were sitting.

'Lawks-a-mussy, wot we got 'ere? A couple o' kids!'

Stefan looked at the girl, perplexed, not understanding a word. She, too, looked blankly at the fierce-looking but not unfriendly figure.

The question put to them by this particular member of the crew was probably a rhetorical one; he would already have been briefed about this pair of irregular passengers. He would also have had an inkling of what was going on in Poland. He and a girlfriend might have seen the film *Dangerous Moonlight* in some smoky cinema while she enjoyed a good cry during the playing of Richard Addinsell's haunting theme tune. He undoubtedly felt genuine sympathy for the two young refugees and had resolved to make their stay aboard as unalarming as possible. They gladly accepted a handful of boiled sweets which he produced from his pocket.

'D' yer speak any English?'

The girl's reply, heavily accented but clear, surprised and impressed him. Then a brief order was barked somewhere further along the now stiflingly hot passageway, and the children's bearded ally quickly disappeared into a jungle of cables, pipes and valves.

Stefan and the girl were left alone for the next hour or so. Then they were invited to get up and follow a member of the crew who told them that the Captain wanted to see them. They scrambled through a series of watertight doors, past a small cage containing two dormant carrier pigeons, and were then shown into a cramped cabin where a naval officer was sitting at a small table covered in charts.

'I'm Lieutenant Irving. I know that you are Polish, and that you speak a little English. You must understand that you are only on board this boat because you happened to arrive from Sweden while we were undergoing emergency repairs near Helsingør. We are making for a port in southern England, where you will be handed over to the British Red Cross. Do you understand?'

The girl nodded.

'Remember that we are on a sea patrol. As long as you do exactly what you are told by members of my crew, you'll be all right.'

He dismissed the two children with a brief smile, and they were led back to their makeshift bed space for'ard.

Stefan was looking forward to going on deck. The girl knew better, and embarked on a series of lessons to introduce the boy to a daunting panoply of English irregular verbs. Meals were brought to them on aluminium plates by crew members. They slept at irregular intervals, unable to differentiate between night and day. Over the next seventy-two hours there was little to break the monotony of steadily throbbing engines, oppressively stale air and minimum movement within the narrow steel hull.

Then one day (or was it night?), the tempo of the diesel engines suddenly slowed, and a few moments later the children felt a gush of cool fresh air on their faces. They sat up expectantly, thinking that their voyage was perhaps at last over. Voices could be heard above the sound of the idling engines, and there was a good deal of movement astern. Suddenly a series of dull explosions shook the whole vessel. This was followed by a loud clattering somewhere above their heads. Orders were shouted, hatches were slammed shut and there was a shuddering surge of power. The girl caught sight of a crew member covered in blood; his eyes were open, but he said nothing, while those around him were yelling.

'Bloody hell, that was one of ours. Quick, get the medic.'

A crew member in dripping oilskins came along to make sure the children were all right. He was surprised at their calm acceptance of what was going on, and would have seen no point in trying to explain to the two young foreigners that an RAF Sunderland flying boat had just mistakenly depth-charged and strafed one of its own submarines. Then their bearded friend appeared, squatted down beside them and told them that everything was OK, there were no German ships or aircraft around and that they would quite soon be docking in England. The girl listened solemnly. She was probably thinking of the new responsibilities that lay ahead of her. As soon as they were alone again she put Stefan through almost two hours of English language revision, until he began to cry with frustration and fatigue. Then they slept.

IV

'Wakey-wakey, yer two young scamps. Time to go ashore.' The familiar bearded figure was towering over them, grinning. ''Ere are yer things – is that the lot?'

The girl stood up unsteadily and checked each item of their light baggage. She pulled Stefan to his feet, and they made their way to a vertical steel ladder and open hatch. Burly arms hoisted them up and out into the fresh air and dazzling sunlight. They were guided along a narrow walkway, stepping carefully over and around jagged flaps of razor-sharp steel which had been peeled off the hull by cannon shells from the earlier air attack. Once clear of the gangplank, they stood still for a moment, mesmerised by all that they heard and saw: formidable grey warships alongside docks bristling with cranes, gantries and anti-aircraft guns; shouting men and revving engines engaged in shifting orderly stacks of stores and munitions; and, of special interest to the girl, various signs stencilled in English. The first of these to catch her eye was fixed to an open-sided van serving hot drinks and buns to a long queue of dockworkers. But even before she could make sense of the words *Salvation Army*, she and Stefan were approached by a brisk middle-aged woman in uniform who announced that she was from the Red Cross and that her name was Mrs de Vries. She would be looking after them for the next leg of their journey.

Without being prompted, Stefan took a step forward, offered his hand and said, 'Good day...*pani*.'

'No, dear. We don't say, "Good day", we say, "How do you do?"' She shepherded them towards an army ambulance parked nearby.

'Did you have a smooth crossing?' she asked, as if the two children had just sauntered ashore from a school outing on a paddle steamer. She did not wait for a reply, and went on to explain that they would be driving from Portsmouth to a small village in Wiltshire where the children would be billeted with a family.

'Come along, get on board. No, no, not that side – we have right-hand drive vehicles in England.'

With Mrs de Vries at the wheel and the two children squeezed together in the passenger seat, they drove through streets where there was a good deal of war damage. Earlier in the year much of the rubble would have been brightened by flourishing rosebay willowherb, dryly nicknamed "bombweed" by dispossessed city dwellers.

'Dreadful, all this bombing.'

The girl made no comment; she had seen very much worse in her native Poland. As they drove north out of the city Stefan and the girl stared out at the close-cropped hills. They had not seen chalk land before.

After a while they pulled into a roadside café. Here Mrs de Vries took the opportunity to give the girl various items which had been issued to her for the two young refugees. These included identity cards, ration books and two small boxes fitted with a strap, each containing a rubbery-smelling gasmask. There was also a Home Office folder, but this was to be passed direct to their host family. They sat down, and the girl was handed a small menu card with half the choices crossed out in thick pencil.

'Now, you choose what you would like for breakfast, and use your best English to order from the waitress.'

The girl frowned and, after a brief glance at the menu, handed it back.

'Righto then, I shall do the honours.'

Soon they were settling down to a sample of the English wartime cooking that would become Stefan's staple diet for many months to come. He devoured everything on his plate. When asked, with a beaming smile, if he was enjoying his bacon turnovers and potato floddies, he nodded enthusiastically, while the girl assumed a dejected expression as she failed to find either "turnover" or "floddy" in her small Polish-English dictionary.

The rest of the journey was, for the two children, an introduction to unprecedented peace and tranquillity. They gazed out at undamaged and picturesque villages with strange pub signs, open fields with grazing sheep and cows, and rolling hills with natural chalk scars. Three years earlier they might have been surprised to see white horses etched into the Wiltshire downs, but these had been turfed over in order to deny distinctive landmarks to errant Luftwaffe pilots. Those few indicators of war which instilled a vague sense of unease in country-dwellers here went unnoticed by Stefan and the girl: recently erected radar towers, the odd prominent building painted in drab camouflage colours, and tactically sited concrete pillboxes with apertures like eyes narrowed against half-expected invasion. And when they stopped for a few minutes in a lay-by on Salisbury Plain the continuous rumble of distant guns firing on the Larkhill artillery ranges caused them less alarm than a sudden explosion of sound from pheasants disturbed in a nearby copse. This perceived remoteness from war lulled them into a strange sense of security, and they slept for the rest of the journey.

As the army ambulance swung round a corner and into a small village called Wilsford, the two children awoke. There was not time to take in the contours and character of the village before they pulled up on a short gravelled driveway in front of a thatched house with white walls.

'Righto, then. Here we are. I'll give you a hand with your luggage.'

The front door of the house opened, and the two children found themselves standing before two incarnations from a half-forgotten schoolbook featuring the English gentry. Major James Standish, dressed stylishly in tweed jacket, woven tie, corduroy trousers and brogues, had seen service in the First World War ("Our War"). He was probably none too pleased to have his pastoral retirement interrupted by another major conflict in Europe. His wife, Ethel, also smartly and sensibly attired, had a rather strident voice and sounded as if she was well in control of events, in and around the house anyway.

After a hasty cup of tea Mrs de Vries revved the army ambulance and departed without ceremony, leaving the two children in the care of their new guardians. The major excused himself and disappeared into the garden to attend to the all-important Home Front business of preparing ground for vegetables. Mrs Standish sat the girl down, and both remained silent while the Home Office file was perused. After a couple of minutes Ethel Standish began speaking slowly and deliberately to the girl, glancing only occasionally at Stefan.

'My husband and I live here with our daughter. Daphne's fiancé is away fighting in the war. You will be sharing the spare bedroom with the little boy until you leave us. In the meantime there are plenty of ways in which you can help me around the house. You speak quite good English, yes?'

The girl nodded, unsmiling.

'Young Stephen' (she anglicised his name without so much as a by-your-leave) 'will need to pick up English as quickly as possible. After Christmas he will be attending a kindergarten in Pewsey.'

The girl winced at the ring of this German-sounding establishment, but was reassured when it was explained to her that the headmistress was a kindly spinster called Miss Bird.

'We'll have supper in an hour. Now let me show you to your room and help you unpack.'

They went upstairs and into a spacious, carpeted bedroom. As soon as the girl snapped open suitcase latches and unbuckled rucksack straps Mrs Standish dived into the children's modest belongings. She was intent on separating clothes for laundering from other items which were to be stowed away tidily in an oak wardrobe and a mahogany military chest. The two children looked on, bemused, as each mundane reminder of their distant Polish home was somehow defiled through exposure and orderly relegation; until, that is, the bottom of the rucksack yielded its dormant secret. Mrs Standish strode across the room, threw open the window and called to her husband who was still down in the vegetable garden.

'James, I think you ought to come up here a moment.'

The major muttered something wearily, and shortly afterwards came shuffling up the stairs. His wife invited him to peer into the rucksack.

'What on earth have we here?'

'Żółw,' replied the girl lamely.

In her confusion the English word "tortoise" had gone completely out of her head. Major Standish took the creature out carefully and lifted it to his nose, sniffing it suspiciously. He then put it down on the dressing table, surprised that it had apparently survived the long journey from Warsaw or wherever.

'It's obviously hibernating. We'd better stick it in a heap of leaves for the rest of the winter.'

All four trooped downstairs and out into the garden where the small creature, intact and unaware inside its shell, was duly dug into its winter quarters.

'Has it got a name?' asked the major.

'Tomasz,' replied the girl.

'Well, there you go, Tom, we'll see you again in the spring.'

The major patted the heap lightly with his garden spade, and the children detected a certain warmth inside the hard English exterior.

As they re-entered the house by the back door, the front door was opened and a cheerful young woman in pullover and corduroy breeches strode in.

''Lo, Mum. I'm home.'

Daphne had been drafted into the Women's Land Army and was now reeking pleasantly enough of silage after a hard day's work on one of the local farms. She smiled at the two children and introduced herself.

'I'm afraid I don't speak a word of Polish. Hope you had a good journey. You must be awfully tired. See you at supper.'

She disappeared upstairs to change.

Throughout supper Stefan ingested wholesome food and English idiom in equal measure. The girl had succeeded in giving him a good grounding in the language. Even though it did not occur to the family to choose their words carefully so as to be better understood by their two young guests (none of the three had a working knowledge of any foreign language), Stefan soon found himself picking up new words and phrases. This, however, involved attentive lip-reading and almost no eye contact. In this way he unconsciously avoided any emotional interplay, enabling him to absorb information all the more readily. This would prove to be an invaluable asset as he strove, over the next few years, to acquire that most elusive of qualities, quintessential Englishness.

V

In the pleasant atmosphere of the room which they were sharing in the Standishs' home, Stefan and the girl started to converse in simple English as a matter of course. She explained to him how to find his way around the dog-eared English elementary grammar book and also how to use the small Polish-English dictionary. And she began adding to the pencilled notes already scribbled in the two books.

Stefan soon settled happily into a new and pleasurable way of life. He liked the food he was given, and he enjoyed freedom to explore the house, garden and the village at large. He responded easily to the friendly curiosity shown towards him by adults and other children alike. And it was not long before he found a kindred spirit at Wilsford House where several families, including evacuees from bombed cities and refugees from abroad, were lodged as paying guests. Feliks Starzyński had escaped from Poland with his father, a colonel in the Polish Army, earlier in the war. He was a studious, bespectacled boy of indeterminate age, his growth having been somewhat stunted in early childhood. Stefan took to Feliks, and was fascinated by his new friend's ingenuity in making ratchety model tanks using old cotton reels, matchsticks, elastic bands and candle wax. Then there was six-year-old Philip at the vicarage who let Stefan play with his treasured Hornby clockwork trains, and would occasionally lead him down to the cellar to gaze at stocks of rations left in the care of the trustworthy clergy in 1940 for emergency distribution in the event of invasion. He also pointed out to him a dummy grave in St Nicholas' churchyard where a cache of small arms and hand grenades were allegedly buried for future use by the Home Guard.

One fine January morning Daphne gave Stefan a special treat. Having borrowed a child's pillion and bolted it on to her bicycle, she sat him in it and they rode off to the farm three miles away where she worked with a team of other felicitous Land Army girls. Under the eagle eye of a still sceptical farmer the young women drove tractors and forked manure off moving trailers and on to recently ploughed fields, while Stefan raced around with a small group of other children, spurred on by all the adult activity around them. At midday everyone sat down together for a brief picnic lunch at the edge of a field. Five German labourers, prisoners of war, sat in a knot on their own while the land girls eyed them, from a distance, with a mixture of suspicion and patriotic disdain. The young women resented the fact that these enemy aliens appeared to be well fed and still defiant. The children, however, with whom the Luftwaffe crewmen sought to ingratiate themselves, hovered around the prisoners, cheerfully exchanging with them uncomprehending chatter and mime. Stefan joined in enthusiastically. He had little idea who these men were, and was mortified when, after carelessly shouting something in Polish, he was deliberately tripped up and then given a surreptitious kick by a glowering prisoner. This vicious little encounter went unnoticed by the chattering land girls.

Suddenly everyone became aware of a steadily increasing roar from a pair of Lancaster bombers which had taken off on a test flight from Boscombe Down. As the dark shapes thundered low overhead the young women and the children cheered and waved, while the Germans stared sullenly at the ground and the farmer frowned at his pocket watch. Then it was all back to work until nightfall.

That evening Stefan went up to bed with a sense of elation. After Daphne had poked her head round the door and bidden them goodnight, he started telling the girl excitedly about all that had happened during the day. But she seemed uninterested. For some weeks Stefan had not seen her at all during the daytime, and when they were reunited at supper she appeared to have withdrawn into herself. Now, even in the sanctuary of the bedroom which they shared, she refused to give him bedtime tuition in English, saying that she needed to sleep. The boy was suddenly aware of something different about her, some deep seasonal change. Total absence of tenderness from his robust and matter-of-fact English hosts had not worried him at all. Other young refugees would later recall, somewhat pathetically, that they had rarely, if ever, received a kiss or fond embrace while living with their adoptive English families. Stefan did not recall any such shows of affection, even before his arrival in England. But this unexpected onset of aloofness on the part of the girl worried him. He lay awake for some time, listening to the creaking of floorboards as people moved about the house, and to the sound of the rising wind outside. Eventually he was lulled to sleep by the now-familiar rumble of guns on the artillery ranges at Larkhill.

VI

By early February Stefan had been enrolled as a pupil at Miss Bird's kindergarten in Pewsey. Miss Bird was stern but scrupulously fair, meting out summary punishment to any child miscreant, regardless of sex or circumstance. Stefan very soon earned the admiration of his classmates by receiving three sharp smacks across the palm of his hand with the headmistress' wooden ruler without even wincing.

By contrast, another foreign child was shown no sympathy whatsoever by her fellow pupils when reduced to tears by Miss Bird's exacting ruler. It was common knowledge that Eva Ziegler, a seven-year-old German Jewish refugee, had lost both parents, one brother and two sisters in Sachsenhausen concentration camp north of Berlin, and had arrived with her host family in Manningford Bruce in a pitiable state. Her mental and psychological recovery had been, by all accounts, remarkable. Within a year she had established herself as a confident and assertive pupil at the small school. Before her arrival there, two teams, each of seven children, would amble each day, in unsupervised crocodile, up to the nearby rectory garden for an hour of outdoor games. Then Eva Ziegler had taken it upon herself to insist that the two teams march in step while she shouted out the time to the compliant but resentful youngsters. At first Stefan could not help but feel a latent and compelling kinship with this melancholy, sallow-skinned waif. But then the pack instinct prevailed, and he readily joined in the infant torment inflicted on her whenever her self-proclaimed authority was seen to wane or be undermined.

Stefan's recent introduction to the English language proved to be no serious handicap to him at the kindergarten. Indeed, he already had a better grasp of elementary grammar than a good number of the other pupils. Even English spelling, the scourge of all newcomers to the language, presented him with fewer problems than one might have expected. This was partly because he was getting used to seeing words in the small Polish-English dictionary entrusted to him by the girl. His pronounced foreign accent went largely unnoticed by the mainly middle-class children in the school, who simply assumed that he was a local Wiltshire boy.

Spring came early in March, and with it the first of two events which would have a profound impact on Stefan's life in his newly adopted country.

He enjoyed the seven-mile journey to and from kindergarten. He got on well with the two children from Marden whose mother received extra petrol coupons to do the daily school run in her old car. He was invariably in good spirits by the time he was dropped off in Wilsford late in the afternoon. After a demanding day at school he would look forward to a quiet half-hour or so doing homework, then a filling meal followed sometimes by simple parlour games with Daphne and her mother. Having a sharp memory, he excelled at Pelmanism, the one-card game that would even draw the girl out of the shadows into which she had unaccountably retreated.

Then one afternoon, on his arrival back from school, he was met by the sight of a large black saloon car in the drive of the Standishs' house. A smartly dressed man and woman were taking their leave of Major Standish, while the girl was helping to load her luggage into the boot of the car. She turned and saw Stefan, and came across to him.

She took him by the shoulders and said earnestly, 'You must continue to improve your English and you must behave well at all times. I have to go now.'

Then she unexpectedly gave him three fleeting kisses, and climbed into the back of the car, which drove off at once. Stefan's slight and sombre guardian had quite suddenly drifted out of his life like a leaf swept away on an icy stream.

He remained rooted to the spot, numbed and dry-eyed. He did not hear Mrs Standish exhorting him to 'Come along now and buck up.' And he remembered nothing thereafter, until the major took him gently by the arm, having found him alone and shivering by the freshly disturbed heap of leaves in the garden.

That night the small boy slid wearily into a dreamless sleep, only to awake in the morning to a new and disquieting, dreamlike solitude. At breakfast he spoke not a word. He only listened, anxious to catch some mention of why and where the girl had gone the day before. Major and Mrs Standish did briefly refer to her journey via London. The boy wondered why, but by then the subject had been changed. Later that day Miss Bird telephoned from the kindergarten to say that Stefan appeared to be under the weather and suggest that he be kept at home for a day or two.

Stefan spent much of the next day alone in his room thumbing through illustrated magazines lent to him by Daphne, and failing to settle down to English language revision for more than a few minutes at a time. No symptoms of sickness emerged and so the following day he was allowed outside again. He made his way at once to Wilsford House to find Feliks, not realising that his friend would be sitting in class at the village school. The sun was out, and he wandered off into the large, rambling garden.

As he made his way across an overgrown grass tennis court and towards the brick boundary wall with a recess and garden seat, he saw a young woman sitting there. He recognised her, in her floral dress, from earlier visits to the house, and eagerly approached her to say hello. But when he had almost reached her he saw that she had covered her face with her hands and was sobbing quietly. He stood gazing at her uncertainly.

Slowly her hands parted across her face, and looking at him through a shimmering veil of tears she said, in a hoarse whisper, 'Please leave me alone. I'm so unhappy. Do you understand? I want to be alone.'

He backed away, turned and headed for the garden gate, innocent of any trespass into the private grief of a twenty-year-old initiate war widow. Only an hour earlier she had received an unimaginable telegram from the Undersecretary of State for War, which deeply regretted to inform her that her husband, Captain Gerald Yates, had been killed in action.

In her immature anguish, there in the sunlit walled garden, she and the Polish boy might have paused to share mutual bewilderment at the inequity of world war. As it was, Stefan had already started lunch with the Standishes, while the major and his wife listened intently to the BBC Home Service on their mahogany-clad wireless. The one o'clock news, read by Alvar Lidell, reported crisply and buoyantly that further successful Allied operations had been carried out against Rommel's Afrika Korps in Tunisia.

Over the next few months Stefan began imperceptibly to shed his Polish identity. His rapid mastery of the English language satisfied Miss Bird and went impressively unnoticed by the Standish family and by the villagers in Wilsford. He readily accepted the vernacular name Stephen, felt comfortable in his "utility" clothes and was frequently and easily persuaded that Great Britain and her Empire were winning the war against Germany.

But then, as time passed, there was a lengthening of hidden shadows. Stephen developed an almost obsessive fear of dogs, even the yapping Chihuahuas and Pekinese cherished by two elderly spinsters in the village. His sleep began to be disturbed by a recurrent nightmare. In this dream he found himself looking up from the bottom of a chalk pit cluttered with undergrowth and a confused mass of something resembling raw meat, and watching a lone figure walking around the edge of the pit, high above him. At the moment when this figure revealed itself as the girl who had abandoned him, he would wake up screaming. The hasty appearance in his room of either Ethel Standish or her daughter could not console him for some minutes. Soothing words were spoken, but neither of the women thought to ask Stephen what was causing him to awake so violently. And so his unspeakable chimaera would continue to haunt him for many nights to come.

He also began to show behavioural changes. When his friend, Philip, proudly showed him a black zero-gauge foreign-made locomotive, with shiny pistons and rectangular smoke deflectors, Stephen set about derailing it with grim satisfaction. Interactive play of almost any kind quickly bored him now. He would turn his attention, instead, to a variety of inanimate objects which began to hold a special fascination for him: fossils and flints yielded up by the Wiltshire chalk hills, cacti basking on south-facing windowsills, and newly minted coins. These evoked no uneasy memories, and possessed a tangible and enduring quality which he found reassuring.

VII

The young widow at Wilsford House, childless and with no perceived hope for the future, grieved for several months. But she gradually began to emerge from a natural season of sorrowing, and by that autumn she was feeling once again in harmony with life around her. She received a series of visits from sympathetic and sensible strangers who, in England at any rate, invariably commend themselves in times of pestilence or war. There was a good deal of soul-searching. Help and advice were freely given and papers were eventually signed. Marion Yates was about to take on a new lease of life, quite literally. Stephen's key role in all this was revealed to him, on return from school late one afternoon, by Ethel Standish.

'Sit down, Stephen. I have something important to tell you.' He fixed his eyes on different objects around the room while she continued, 'You know Mrs Yates at Wilsford House whose husband was killed in action earlier in the year? Well, she was very unhappy to be left on her own, and she has decided that she would like to adopt a child.'

'Adopt?' asked Stephen.

'She would like to take a child and look after him as her own.'

'That will be nice for her,' said the boy blandly.

Mrs Standish prevaricated almost frantically for several more minutes, rambling on about the exceptional circumstances of the war, the misfortune of children, especially those from foreign countries, who had lost their parents, and the importance of a settled and secure childhood. She was rapidly drifting away from the very point of her conversation with Stephen, when he quite unexpectedly threw her a lifeline.

'Does Mrs Yates want me to be her child?'

Ethel Standish beamed with relief. She honestly believed that the small boy's words had been spoken from the heart. She did not understand that his turbulent early years had taught him an unusual degree of pragmatism and openness to sound ideas.

And so Stephen became, to all intents, Marion Yates' son, the assumption having been made by the adoption agency that she would remarry soon after the end of the war. His new mother was unstinting in her love, a commendably robust love engendered by wartime stoicism and endurance. Creature comforts were scarce, and overt shows of affection were also strictly rationed. But once Marion and Stephen had moved to Manningford to live under the same roof as her ageing parents, she would spare no effort on the boy's behalf. His education at the kindergarten in Pewsey continued uninterrupted. She introduced him to other families with children. And, thinking ahead to the purchase of Christmas and birthday presents for her new young son, she resolved to set aside, from then on, any coins bearing the date 1943.

Marion Yates was by now aware of the financial problems which would arise as Stephen grew up. Accordingly, she wasted no time in approaching local grant-making trusts and other benefactors to secure the continuing private education which she felt would be good for him. Her parents could not spare any money but were generous in their advice on Stephen's education and upbringing. Stephen's adoptive grandfather, a somewhat choleric retired brigadier who had served with distinction in the First World War and subsequently for many years in Africa and India, soon established an easy and robust relationship with the boy. They would sit together looking through periodicals graphically covering various British campaigns of the 1914–1918 war. The old brigadier would sometimes utter remarks which betrayed a profound and enduring loathing of the Germans.

As the months passed, Stephen's recurrent bad dream became less frequent and his destructive tendencies less obscure. Any unruly behaviour on his part arose, rather, from his association with other children. He and an extrovert boy called Alexander pursued mild mischief together, roaming around Manningford armed with tin toy pistols which fired raw potato pellets. They derived particular amusement from harassing a mentally disturbed and half-starved family living near the main railway line. One of these hapless people, named Edgar Mullen, cut a disconsolate and sinister figure. He was very tall, and had gangling arms and a haunted face with sunken cheeks and eyes set deep in their sockets. He was always dressed in a long black overcoat, flat cap and heavy army boots, and he was in the habit of springing almost noiselessly up and down without, apparently, bending his knees. The two boys sensed something darkly challenging, and delighted in taking pot shots at him with their potato guns and, occasionally, pelting him with small stones before running away laughing. They might have been more hesitant had they realised how abnormally strong the deranged young man was. One or two alarmed villagers had actually witnessed him lifting up a heavy iron drain grating with one hand and heaving it effortlessly over the hedge, but then poor Edgar had never actually harmed anyone.

For reasons which he would not admit, even to himself, Stephen took care to avoid Eva Ziegler when out and about in the village. However, she had by this time gathered her own small circle of friends unconnected with Miss Bird's kindergarten. Had the two children been on speaking terms they might have discovered a mutual area of unspectacular prejudice against them. On more than one occasion Eva had ambled home barefoot, having had her shoes forcibly removed and thrown into the stream by children from a prominent local Catholic family.

For Stephen, disapprobation in the name of the church was somewhat subtler. As a regular Anglican churchgoer, Marion had confided in the vicar of Manningford Bruce, and Stephen Yates was made politely welcome at church services. He was also enrolled as a member of the Sunday school. Here the children were issued with small paperback albums into which they would stick large stamps depicting different biblical themes. Stephen was excluded, on the pretext of language difficulties, from any discussion or re-enactment of New Testament stories. And he did not receive any of the biblical stamps because, he was told, there were not quite enough to go round, and in any case his was alphabetically the last name on the children's register. Stephen enjoyed Sunday school nonetheless, and picked up some useful lessons on how to shape up as a passable Christian in his new homeland.

As time passed, and the war in Europe came to an end, Marion Yates could afford to give Stephen one shilling a week for pocket money. He dutifully hoarded these coins in a wooden cigar box discarded by the old brigadier, and was reluctant to spend them, especially the newly minted ones. The only things he budgeted for were small accessories for a Meccano set which he had inherited, and books which he would purchase from a bookshop on the High Street in Marlborough. He was already an avid reader, fascinated as much by the literary style as by the content of his burgeoning library. He found pleasure in the very sound of many English words, particularly where these contrasted onomatopoeically with their already fading Polish equivalents. "Bird" and "butterfly" suggested infinitely freer flight than "*ptak*" and "*motyl*"; it seemed to him that a "flower" was much more for a plant to rejoice in than "*kwiat*", and that "wedding" had a distinctly more magical ring about it than "*ślub*". He delighted in reading poetry and would recite nursery rhymes and traditional children's verse over and over again in his mind. And he would always listen intently to adult conversation around him.

VIII

An extraordinary event one summer afternoon narrowly failed to impose yet another dramatic change of direction in Stephen's early life. Marion Yates was driving her father to Devizes in her sluggish second-hand car when, at a spot know as Marden Clump, a salvo of twenty-five-pounder artillery shells exploded beside the main road on which they were travelling. Blast from the first round caused the windscreen and nearside windows of the car to shatter simultaneously. The old brigadier flung open the nearside door, dragging his deafened and bewildered daughter into a shallow ditch beside the road, while seven more shells exploded around them.

Once the firing had stopped they returned to the car to find that one piece of shrapnel had struck the metal pillar beside the front passenger seat and ricocheted out through the rear window. Had Stephen not misbehaved earlier that day and so been left at home with the "daily", he would have been sitting behind and between the two front seats and directly in the path of this shell fragment.

It transpired later that an error on the gun line at Larkhill had been responsible for an initial salvo being fired almost one mile outside the artillery range danger area. The War Office awarded Marion Yates eighty pounds by way of compensation for her ordeal. Every so often she would allow Stephen to open her jewellery box, and there among the bracelets, brooches and rings lay a jagged sliver of shrapnel which had been gouged out of the bodywork of her fatefully protective Morris Eight.

Destiny had plotted a different course for Eva Ziegler. Late one August she was reported missing from home, after running off to watch a small RAF trainer aircraft practising forced landings on the grass airstrip on Manningford Bohune Common. Her scarcely identifiable body was discovered a few days later, sprawled in dense undergrowth beside the railway line. Her skull had been crushed by a cast-iron drain grating found lying close by. No one had noticed the coincidental disappearance of Edgar Mullen. It was not until October, when the trees had lost their leaves, that his decaying remains were spotted, by a group of children, hanging in Frith Copse.

The sudden absence of these two obscurely malign influences in Stephen's life was both opportune and wholesome. By the time he had started at a boys' preparatory school in Dorset he had shed his aggressive tendencies, regained his aptitude for making friends and unconsciously remodelled his stilted English.

Five years at the small private boarding school in the Isle of Purbeck were halcyon days for Stephen. The teaching staff there consisted of a close-knit team of benign martinets who had been either too old or too unfit for military service during the war. Discipline, both behavioural and academic, was non-negotiable.

A considerable amount of English spelling, Latin grammar and French syntax had to be learned by rote. And even a minor infringement of school rules, such as dropping a sweet paper, could earn the unlucky offender a painful beating. The old maxim *Mens sana in corpore sano* was applied with zeal. Almost total immersion in a cold bath before breakfast was the order of the day, and every afternoon was devoted to sport. Stephen soon learned the honour, even the masochistic pleasure, of minor injury in the boxing ring or on the rugby pitch. Nakedness, a prevalent feature of the school's fitness regime, no longer caused him vicarious anxiety. The other boys were unembarrassed by their own, or others', nudity. And only one member of the staff, who was later to leave under a cloud, might have made a prurient distinction between Gentile and Jew at the school swimming pool or in the boys' communal shower.

Stephen thrived on the many and varied extramural activities organised to engender traditional moral values and develop character. Daily worship and compulsory Bible-reading just before lights-out introduced him comfortably to church music and to an archaic form of English which he found poetic and appealing. Jam jars filled with leaves standing in odd corners of classrooms and dormitories contained brightly coloured and tufted caterpillars collected during walks to and from sea swimming at Dancing Ledge. A couple of glass showcases in the music practice room displayed fossils and prehistoric flint tools picked up during supervised expeditions to Lulworth Cove. During these excursions discipline and diligence gave way to free-range enjoyment and frivolity. One of the staff was both an amateur palaeontologist and a master of the conundrum.

'Why did the ducks go into the pond? For divers reasons. And why did they come out of the pond? For sun-dry reasons!'

Stephen admired the capacity of the English language for being all at once clever and quirky.

The sterner world outside the mellow stone walls of the school was selectively brought into focus for the boys through notable events. With the death of King George VI in February 1952, and then the coronation of Queen Elizabeth the following year, much was made of the continuity of the British Empire, represented by extensive areas of pink on world maps which graced the classroom walls. Mercator's projection perfectly highlighted this colossal sphere of influence of which Stephen and his peers were taught to be inordinately proud. Then there was a memorable day out to visit the Spithead Coronation Review in June 1953. Several weeks had already been spent poring over illustrated brochures showing the position of each vessel at anchor in the review. As the local paddle steamer on which they were crowded chugged between seemingly endless lines of towering grey warships of every class and nationality the youngsters launched into paroxysms of patriotic pride or defiance. The Soviet cruiser, Sverdlov, a menacing and forbidden incarnation of the Cold War, drew particularly fierce fire from Stephen and his friends.

Not long after this excursion an incident occurred, on a beach near Swanage, which afforded another sombre reminder of the seam-less progression from post-war recovery to planning and preparation for World War III. While a low-flying Lockheed Neptune maritime reconnaissance aircraft on a training flight was dropping anti-sub-marine sonar devices into the sea off Durlston Head an organised party of boys from a neighbouring school were walking along the sands, when three of them were noticed lingering behind the others and then attacking a metal object with a shoehorn and penknife. The hefty explosion which followed killed all three instantaneously. The culprit was later confirmed as a severely corroded anti-tank mine which had failed to be cleared from the beach at the end of the war, and which had been exposed by recent storms. For some days Stephen and his friends engaged in animated discussion about how the three victims would have been blown to pieces. The reality was every bit as distressing. One pair of grieving parents were actually left with nothing whatsoever for burial.

IX

Within the hallowed confines of his preparatory school Stephen became steadily more proficient in a host of worthy activities. He gave a good account of himself in contact sports, which demanded more grit than skill. And he surprised even his own piano teacher by winning a winter music competition with a spirited performance of a Chopin mazurka. By the age of twelve his academic attainment in a wide range of traditional subjects, including Latin and classical Greek, guaranteed him easy entry into one of the country's top public schools. This imposing Victorian pile in Berkshire had a reputation for turning out career soldiers and diplomats, and ran a generous endowment scheme for educating the sons of war widows.

School life for Stephen now became physically and socially more challenging. While each boy enjoyed the relative privacy of a partitioned room, the prevailing ethos of the school was one of fervent group involvement and team loyalty. A rigid code of discipline was enforced for its own sake, it seemed. Failure to empty a wastepaper basket by six o'clock in the evening could result in a caning by one of the prefects. Rules were never questioned by the boys, and the staff turned a blind eye to some unpleasant roughhouse activities which were judged to be character-building. Stephen only once intervened, after a junior boy had been locked in his own school trunk and then trundled down four flights of stairs during the end-of-term revelries, but as soon as death by asphyxia had been ruled out, Stephen joined in the hilarity of seeing the young claustrophobe lying beside his open trunk, convulsed with terror and shock.

Illicit copies of the *Kama Sutra* and Vladimir Nabokov's *Lolita* which were being breathlessly circulated around the school barely caught his attention, let alone his imagination. Books on modern history, on the other hand, absorbed much of his spare time. The 1950s were already spawning literature about the less heroic and more contentious aspects of the Second World War. Stephen learned for the first time of the political cynicism and treachery which underlay many of the military campaigns still being exalted in briskly compiled official war histories.

He was puzzled by contemporary accounts of Poland's relentless role as victim, successively, of German aggression, Soviet exploitation and Western Allied indifference. Only many years later would mature reflection ignite in him a sense of outrage at the tardily chronicled circumstances surrounding some of the most fateful events of the war: the Nazi-Soviet Pact; the execution of more than four thousand Polish officers by the Soviet Union's NKVD at Katyń; and then the Allied conferences at Tehran, Yalta and Potsdam which presumed, among other things, to map out the course of history for another whole generation of Poles.

But even now he reflected more than once on something his

childhood friend, Feliks Starzyński, had told him during a brief return visit to Wilsford. Feliks' father had been looking forward to the grand victory parade staged in London on 8th June 1946. However, for the sake of appeasing Great Britain's erstwhile ally and imminent arch-enemy, the Soviet Union, Polish heroism and sacrifice in the service of the British Armed Forces had been ungratefully spurned; the government of the day had refused to allow any of those Polish servicemen to take part. Even at the age of seven, this had struck Stephen as an act of disloyalty completely at odds with what he already understood to be a sacrosanct British sense of fair play.

X

Memories can be disturbing, but partial oblivion even more so. For no obvious reason the right-hand cuffs of Stephen's woollen pullovers invariably frayed early, causing finger-size holes to appear in the lower sleeve. At his previous school this had been no more than a minor problem of wear and tear. But now these inconsequential unravellings stirred such sorrow in the robustly maturing boy that he would suddenly find himself sobbing involuntarily. Then he would quickly pull himself together and get on with the business of growing up in the holistic way that was expected of him.

The college chapel was central to the organisation and ethos of the school. Stephen felt at ease with the set routine of daily morning services, compline one evening per week and Sunday services which saw six hundred boys file into chapel for both matins and evensong. During sermons and readings Stephen would idly spot friends in the tiered pews across the nave, and then let his eye move up to the tall stained-glass windows high above the altar. These depicted a mosaic of oddly juxtaposed images, among them a pelican drawing its own blood to nourish its young, and an oncoming steam railway locomotive which seemed to be bearing down remorselessly on the unprayerful.

During school holidays Stephen was taken, with Marion Yates' blessing, under the patrician wing of the owner of the manor house in Manningford Bruce. As the father of three young daughters with little enthusiasm for outdoor pursuits he welcomed the opportunity to introduce Stephen to two particular skills. The boy immediately recognised these as not just manly but irresistibly potent.

Horsemanship wholly absorbed him for the best part of three summers. The sturdy piebald cob which he was taught to ride was no thoroughbred; nor did Stephen emerge as a born equestrian. And yet the primeval covenant between man and beast strongly appealed to him. Even the mundane preliminaries played keenly on those senses which were heightened with the onset of adolescence. The distinctive smell of saddlery and animal sweat was starkly evocative. Rubbing down and curry-combing the muscular animal brought him to a focused awareness of texture, physique and pent-up energy. And once in the saddle, Stephen became aware of the strength to be gained from venturing boldly beyond mere self-reliance.

The second skill which Stephen acquired with the encouragement of his tweedy patron was, by contrast, highly individualistic but no less compelling, and one in which he displayed a natural aptitude. Grey sherds strewn across the meadow behind the manor house testified to his early successes in clay pigeon shooting. And his marksmanship with the .22 calibre rifle yielded a large tinful of misshapen copper pennies which had been hit from a range of some twenty yards. He found the explosive convergence of mastery and metal on a distant target consummately rewarding.

*

Even in his final year Stephen managed to cope well with the fiercely repressive demands of public school life. It never seriously occurred to him to secretly drink or smoke. His closest friendships with other boys were fraternal and uncomplicated. And nubile young women, being wholly out of sight, remained largely out of mind.

With self-discipline and increased acceptance of responsibility came the dawning of a desire to be an achiever. After sitting a series of taxing university entrance exams, he finally gained a place at Oxford. He revelled for a while in measured self-esteem and a heady optimism. Striving towards an honours degree would surely mark the end of Orphic retrospection and enable him to turn away, once and for all, from his now distantly svelte and singular loss.

In his last term at the school he and his fellow sixth-formers were given the task of performing a satirical revue to be delivered entirely in German. The guest of honour was to be a middle-ranking representative from the West German Embassy in London, by the name of Oskar Szyller. Having recently tackled Friedrich Schiller's *Wallenstein* for German A Level, Stephen was struck by the spelling of the German Second Secretary's surname, but then gave the matter no further thought as he set about learning his lines and rehearsing for his debut on the school stage.

He had two short performances to act out. The second of these was a stilted monologue which required him to brave the footlights wearing a dirndl and blonde wig with coiled plaits. The embroidered dress was an improvised outfit borrowed from his housemaster's squarely built sixteen-year-old daughter who had apparently just discovered cheap perfume. It was in this Heidi-like and suggestively redolent costume that Stephen was formally introduced to Herr Szyller after the final curtain. The German diplomat complimented Stephen unsmilingly on his fluent performance and passed on. Then, as he was being ushered out to his embassy chauffeur-driven car, he turned briefly back to Stephen.

'And now are you proposing to join the Diplomatic Service or perhaps the Armed Forces when you will have left school?'

Stephen replied that this would depend on what degree he gained at university. Herr Szyller nodded, shook him by the hand and departed. Stephen, still feeling awkward and absurd in his virginal stage costume, was nevertheless flattered that the distinguished visitor should have expressed even a passing interest in his future career.

XI

During the ten months between leaving school and going up to Oxford, Stephen earned his first modest salary teaching German and French for two terms at a disconcertingly unruly independent school near Romsey. The job was not demanding and he found ample time to extend his reading. He became fascinated by the way in which the sheer subtlety of the English language revealed itself in modern poetry. Slim volumes containing the poems of unpretentious English and Australian contemporary writers enthralled him no less than the collected works of the pre-eminent nineteenth and twentieth-century English-speaking poets. But for him the very language of much poetry still transcended the ideas which it strove to express. The words themselves captivated him.

Military history, particularly that emerging from the two world wars, engendered in Stephen a faintly perverse admiration for the German nation; its inexorable rise to power and supremacy while the rest of Europe revelled, its undeniable claim to military prowess in war and its monolithic stoicism in eventual defeat. The dark forces of Nazism had been so comprehensively vilified in the aftermath of the war that many young men of Stephen's generation instinctively shrank from further unqualified censure. Harrowing details about the wartime extermination camps in Germany and Poland were now being published in affordable paperbacks illustrated with tantalisingly few and indistinct photographs. Like many of his contemporaries, Stephen was briefly and morbidly fascinated. But the enormity of those crimes against people like himself remained grimly monochrome, out of focus and remote.

Early undergraduate days lived up to Stephen's expectations. The whole concept of an intimate and focused tutorial system appealed strongly to him. This was, after all, academic privilege at its best. However, he was puzzled by his respective tutors' lack of insistence on the writing of refined English. Most of the undergrads at his college were from Welsh working-class backgrounds. They had got into Oxford by dint of sharp intellect and ruthlessly hard work. They were rightly and aggressively proud of their scholastic status. But when it came to reading out their essays at fortnightly tutorials, original thinking and intelligent analysis seemed to Stephen to be diminished by poorly constructed sentences and even misuse of English, and yet this was invariably overlooked. It would take Stephen some time to understand that he was wasting much intellectual effort in producing carefully composed written work at the expense of groundbreaking ideas.

In-depth study of German and French literature sharpened Stephen's interest in modern European history. On the one hand it reinforced his recognition of French culture as exquisite, overwhelmingly presumptuous and nationally self-absorbing. On the other hand, and of more interest to him, it shed some light on the dark origins and even darker consequences of the German psyche. His Yorkshire-born German tutor in college amused him on one occasion by declaring baldly that all Germans were fundamentally barbarian. It occurred to Stephen that the French intelligentsia could be forgiven for thinking the same of the eminently terrestrial Anglo-Saxons. But a growing insight into German literature and the arts yielded something inescapably sinister about a mid-European tribe which had nailed Varus' mighty legions to trees in the Teutoburger Wald; and a nation which, almost two thousand years later, had brought destruction on an unprecedented scale to the civilised world. What were these deeply disturbed forces of nature which seemed capable of overriding philosophical, and even rational, thought? They imbued Wagnerian opera with something irresistibly majestic, only to echo away into black forests and opaque myth. They had surfaced alarmingly, but had been historically short-lived, in the political diatribes of Adolf Hitler and his fanatical adherents. What really struck Stephen, though, was the realisation that they had also impinged on the intellects of some of Germany's greatest artists and men of letters. Even the sophisticated genius of figures like Dürer and Goethe was not, it seemed, immune from an unsettling preoccupation with a whole gamut of primitive and uncommonly dangerous ideas.

Late one evening Stephen was enjoying a lively discussion about introspective French and German nineteenth-century poets with a fellow modern linguist, Rowan Pugh, when the latter came out with the remark, 'Hell, Steve. If I really had to choose between those two human conditions, give me ennui rather than angst any day!'

Stephen chuckled at this tacit and terse indictment of two

contrary cultures. He relished a language which borrowed foreign words to distance its own people from other nations' neuroses.

'I entirely agree with you, Rowan. Whereas ennui generally develops into mere malaise, this angst thing seems to lead invariably to putsch, blitzkrieg and schadenfreude!'

The two young men laughed raucously, topped up their glasses with plonk and turned their conversation to girls.

'I must introduce you to Melanie Sledge sometime,' said Rowan. 'She's one of the few women reading chemistry at St Hilda's. She comes over here for tutorials. I think you'll like her.'

XII

While Stephen had been progressing uneventfully from boyhood to manhood the Cold War had been intensifying. In the autumn of 1956 there was scant Western press coverage of Moscow's political and military intervention in Poland following the workers' strike in Poznań. But in November of that year the whole world was able to watch the ruthless suppression of the Hungarian Uprising using thirty thousand Soviet troops supported by tanks. Just one year later the Soviets' successful launch into orbit of a twenty-two-inch diameter satellite sent cosmic shock waves through the West. On his way to spend a holiday improving his German at the home of a family in Austria, Stephen had eagerly photographed this spherical prodigy, barely bigger than a beach ball, while it was on display at the Universal Exhibition in Brussels. At that time he and most of his young friends, not conversant with the complex technology of the space race, were sceptical about the global threat posed by a faintly bleeping sputnik, just as they were unconvinced by current Civil Defence survival pamphlets which invited householders all over Britain to use bookcases packed with earth to barricade their homes against imminent nuclear attack.

Then, on 1st May 1960, even as Moscow was staging one of its most spectacular May Day parades to date, an American U-2 spy plane piloted by Gary Powers was shot down at some enormous altitude over the Soviet Union. Political outrage on both sides of the Iron Curtain ensued. But by the time Powers had been theatrically repatriated, in exchange for a Soviet master spy, on the Glienicke Bridge between West Berlin and Potsdam two major crises had brought the world another step closer to nuclear annihilation. The erection of the Berlin Wall in August 1961 and the Cuban missile crisis which broke the following year were, by any standards, stupendous events which impacted powerfully on Stephen's generation of young ideologues. The compassionate and the faint-hearted rallied convivially behind the banners of the Campaign for Nuclear Disarmament. Many more young men and women, Stephen among them, resigned themselves soberly to the prevailing realpolitik of the day.

Sobriety was not the hallmark of the Oxford University Officers' Training Corps Mess, of which Stephen became a member in his second year. He was surprised, therefore, by the quality of army training on offer by the OTC. His room in college was soon littered with stereoscopic pairs of unclassified air photographs issued to officer cadets for training as potential photo interpreters.

Then the OTC Intelligence Section sent him, for the first week of the winter vacation, on a resistance-to-interrogation course somewhere in Scotland. The canvas canopy of the army truck transporting the course students for the last fifty miles of the journey remained firmly secured until they arrived, under cover of darkness, at a remote snow-covered camp. This godforsaken place was being run by stony-faced men and women dressed in Eastern Bloc uniforms or equally un-English civilian attire. The training that followed was rigorous and clearly professional. Stephen was intensely interested and impressed. He was also amused that reveille at five o'clock each morning was played by an unmistakeably Scottish piper marching up and down between the rows of freezing Nissen huts. On his return journey to Oxford he reflected on the failure of an acquaintance of his to be accepted into the OTC, simply on account of his Finnish parentage.

When he arrived back at college late that evening, lugging a heavy army kitbag, he was astonished to find Melanie Sledge waiting for him in his room. He had only taken her out once since being introduced to her by Rowan Pugh, and was expecting her to have gone away for the winter "vac".

'Hello, how did you know when I'd be back?'

He resisted the urge to ask how she had got his room key from the porter's lodge, or indeed why she was there at all.

'Simple, darling – I telephoned your adjutant.'

'You what?'

'I just rang up the dashing Captain Whittaker.'

Right now Stephen did not much appreciate her flippant and high-handed manner. He had taken his specialist training in Scotland seriously. Two days of enforced sleep deprivation had exhausted him, and he was in no mood for a late-night tête-à-tête with a woman he hardly knew.

She ran her fingers through her tousled fair hair, smiled languidly and asked, 'Aren't you going to offer me a drink?'

Stephen reluctantly poured her a small beer from a can, and was surprised how quickly she emptied her glass. He joined her for her second beer and slowly started to feel less edgy.

They discussed their respective courses of study for a while. But Melanie was curious to learn more of Stephen himself, and began to quiz him about his family background. She curled up comfortably in his other armchair and listened in silence as he started, hesitantly, to talk about his wintery arrival in England at the age of four. This was the first time he had spoken to anyone about that early part of his life, and already he wished he hadn't. He promptly steered the conversation towards his privileged English upbringing and education, but Melanie would not be sidetracked.

'How extraordinary to have been brought all the way from Poland, in the middle of the war, by another child. Who was she? Was she your sister? What was her name? What happened to her?'

Almost without thinking, Stephen replied wearily, 'You know I am not required to answer these questions.' Then, laughing apologetically, he said, 'I'm sorry, but I honestly don't know the answers.'

Melanie persisted. 'Well, what was she like?'

'Thin,' he murmured vacantly.

She dropped to the floor from her armchair, and sat at Stephen's feet.

'Thin? What you mean, thin? Good grief, Steve! Is that really all you can remember?'

Stephen said nothing. Then, quickly regaining his poise, he began to ask Melanie Sledge about her own family.

'Well, I have to tell you that my mother's a broad Scot and an unrepentant divorcee. She met my father early on in the war when he came to Britain to escape the Nazis. I can only just remember him. Shortly after I was born the family name was anglicised to make life easier all round.'

At this point the penny dropped. Stephen glanced at her knowingly, and asked, 'So why aren't you called Melanie Herring?'

She feigned annoyance, slapped him playfully on the leg and exclaimed, 'Hey! I thought you said some time ago that you'd forgotten all your Polish.' She paused. 'Well, it seems to me that you and I have something quite interesting in common.'

Stephen did not share her sense of intrigue, and felt relieved when his plausible intruder finally stood up to leave. She was travelling to Inverness by train the next day and had an early morning start ahead of her. She gave him a condescending peck on the cheek and departed.

Stephen slept feverishly that night. Melanie Sledge, née Śledź, did not feature in his disjointed and troubled dreams.

XIII

In his final year at Oxford Stephen immersed himself in fresh interests and activities which insidiously drew him away from serious academic study.

He spent idle hours on the River Cherwell gondoliering a crudely restored punt which he and a colleague had bought for just ten pounds at the beginning of their second year. Sultry summer afternoons drifting along in the company of Melanie Sledge, and other more glamorous but less astute young females, evoked in Stephen a peculiar nostalgia for something which he had never actually experienced. But he enjoyed even more the novelty of scaling a side wall of the college just before dawn and joining two other third year undergrads for stealthy punting expeditions to illegally shoot duck some way upstream from Parson's Pleasure.

He began writing poetry; obsessively well crafted verses which revealed an exultant mastery of the English language, some highly original thinking but nothing whatsoever of his deepest emotions. Thanks to years of studied self-discipline and restraint these remained securely inaccessible, even to him.

Fired with a growing enthusiasm for things military, Stephen eagerly accepted an invitation, through the university OTC, to go on a Territorial Army parachute course, shortly before sitting his finals. The folly of this decision did not occur to him once during his ten days at RAF Abingdon. Here he was quick to recognise the efficacy of training which focused wholly on technique, and which diminished both fear and thrill well before the course students actually started parachuting; first from an eerily silent tethered balloon, and then from a hideously unwieldy and thunderous Blackburn Beverley heavy transport aircraft. He admired the detached professionalism of the Parachute Regiment instructors and RAF aircrew alike. And he enjoyed the brief comradeship of an aloof young TA officer of the SAS. This maverick on the course twice narrowly avoided arrest by the Oxfordshire police by beating them to the main gate of the airfield in his well-tuned TR-2 sports car, and yet he would invariably be vomiting within seconds of take-off for the dropping zone fifteen miles away. Here, in his way, was the personification of triumph over adversity.

On the cloudless morning that Stephen made his eighth, and qualifying, jump over Weston-on-the-Green a dishevelled young woman was sunning herself on a grassy knoll overlooking the disused airfield. It would not have been clear to the casual observer which was of more interest to her: a pair of unconventional black parachute canopies being trialled by two of the course instructors, or an unobtrusive car with Eastern Bloc diplomatic number plates apparently having its wheel changed in a lay-by adjacent to the perimeter fence.

The army was slow to send Stephen a certificate recording his successful completion of the parachute course. It arrived, four months later, on the same day that he was informed by letter that he had been awarded a predictably disappointing second-class honours degree in German and French. The Senior Branch of the Foreign Service, for which he had by this time sat written exams and undergone gruelling interviews in London, had not been impressed.

The appearance of his name near the top of a published list of unsuccessful candidates was duly noted by Oskar Szyller. The undervalued West German diplomat of Polish extraction by now felt ideologically comfortable passing low-level information to his opposite number at the embassy of the German Democratic Republic in Belgrave Square.

XIV

Stephen's decision to apply for a regular commission in the army was taken after only brief reflection. In recent years the military ethos had begun to appeal strongly to his innate sense of honour and deeply ingrained respect for authority, and he was attracted by the notion of the "regimental family" fostered by the infantry county regiment which he now aspired to join.

His acceptance into the regiment of his choice was little more than a formality. To no obvious military purpose the army was currently in hot pursuit of university graduates. The Regular Commissions Board at Westbury gave undue weight to the qualifications which Stephen had gained while in his university OTC. Generous pass marks were awarded to him barely before he had finished tackling some of the obstacles and command tasks designed to identify potential officers. At Tidworth Military Hospital both his knees jerked obligingly when tapped smartly with a reflex-testing hammer, and the Medical Board accepted his assurance that he was not a habitual sleepwalker. Within a week he was reporting for duty with his regiment in the West Country.

The battalion, which was preparing to deploy to the Far East for operational service in Borneo, had little reason to welcome a newly commissioned officer as yet untrained for command and therefore dangerously inexperienced in the art of war. However, his unpretentious attitude, his eagerness to learn and, curiously, the small parachute badge on his sleeve; all these stood him in good stead. Stephen Yates was given the benefit of the doubt, and sent on two intensive platoon commanders' courses in quick succession. Both focused wholly on the anticipated war in North-West Europe.

Within days of the battalion arriving in its new barracks in Singapore, Stephen and his platoon of thirty-six soldiers found themselves at the Jungle Warfare School in Ulu Tiram, up-country in Malaysia. Here he was surprised to feel in his element. Since early childhood he had frequently alarmed adults by inadvertently stealing up on them without a sound. His natural ability to move silently and surreptitiously quickly emerged as a shadowy asset in the rainforests of this vast training area. His soldiers were mildly disappointed that their young platoon commander was not out of the stable of the landed gentry, like many of the officers in the regiment, and they were suspicious of his obvious lack of experience in command. But they trained hard to emulate his small-arms marksmanship and his uncanny stealth, even in dense secondary jungle.

Throughout the ten months of intensive training that followed, often under the aegis of Australian Army instructors, Stephen developed a profound affinity with the jungle. Here he could not have been further from the complexities of fast-moving mechanised training for all-out war on the North German Plain. Deep shadows cast by the jungle canopy obscured and softened uncomfortably divided feelings for his distantly native Poland. When the long nights drew in, and fallen leaves began to glow mysteriously on the jungle floor, even his most toughened soldiers seemed to him to become lost in their own thoughts. He knew that they must be wondering whether all this training would prove its worth on their first encounter with a live enemy in Borneo. He watched, reflected and made mental notes which would later crystallise into restrained and tentative verse:

Like corrugated iron they ripple on.
The resonant Australian voices claim
That lost or sick, half-starving or bewildered,
We only need to look about to see
That the jungle's an immense dispensary,
A map of the map, "a bloody great green salad".

No one doubts we can and will survive;
Survive the swamp which swallows up our sweat,
Outlive our thin chameleon uniforms
Torn on the insistent "waitawhile",
Break the belukar,
Curse and hack, break out of the belukar,
Survive that first ambush,
Thought of, dreamed of, seen in detail, sprung;
Recreated long before it happens.
It is so easy.

All this is just a choice 'twixt life and death,
A trial of strength, an appeal to reflexes.
But in the last light of a jungle base camp
The quiet and peacefulness are relative.
Slender plants and saplings shake and quiver
As raindrops splash from the living canopy.
The fallen leaves begin to phosphoresce,
Diminutive portents of an afterlife.
Cold consciences are dimly preyed upon
By an ill-defined, translucent form of fear
Like palely frosted glass before the moon
Standing between ourselves and certainty.

I think an artist might depict this wraith,
Stalking between these men and the tall trees,
As something cerebral in casual spaces,
A shadow with depth, a face among the faces.

But the ghosts which visited Stephen in that uneasy tranquillity were more personal and persistent than the demons which taunted his soldiers. At the feverish onset of tropical night he would be confronted by faces to which he could not even put names: a stern patriarchal figure with the immobile features of a portrait photograph; a tall, gaunt woman who ceaselessly mouthed inaudible words; and then the first person in his life whom he could remember for sure, the girl who had brought him out of some unspeakable purgatory, only to abandon him on the threshold of a new language and a new life. In his dreams, or semi-wakefulness, her image would suddenly come fully into focus. But the eyes that looked straight into his own were now dark and reproachful. Then, as her face came ever closer to his, he would recoil involuntarily and jerk awake, unheard.

The so-called confrontation with the Indonesian Army in Borneo came to an abrupt end shortly before the battalion had completed its jungle warfare training. Stephen and his soldiers would not, after all, have the opportunity to put their specialist skills to the ultimate test. They now had to prepare for an indeterminate period of garrison life in West Germany, retraining and preparing for Armageddon.

XV

Stephen's familiar rainforest world evaporated on his next posting. This was to another battalion of the regiment, stationed in
a picturesque provincial town in North-Rhine Westphalia, one
hundred miles from the Inner German Border. He adjusted to his
new role with a mixture of enthusiasm and unease. Here he was,
at last, on the front line in the Cold War. Winter border patrols
gave him his first sight of East German frontier troops observing
and photographing his every move from concrete watchtowers sited
along linear minefields and avenues of barbed wire which stretched
away into the fog. He and his brother officers received periodic
briefings based on information from intelligence sources which
remained loftily anonymous. Top secret code words triggered off
rapid practice deployments to tactical "hides" on expected Soviet
axes of advance across the IGB.

As Stephen's under-crewed armoured personnel carriers clattered
due eastwards across the sleeping German countryside just before
midnight one Friday, he grimly appreciated the need for worst-
case planning. A full-scale Soviet surprise attack over a weekend,

let alone on New Year's Eve, would catch at least thirty per cent of his soldiers unfit through drink or closeted with fatalistic young Fräuleins. Meanwhile the battalion's families had been issued with standing instructions stressing the futility of trying to make their way westwards, together with several million other refugees, at the outbreak of hostilities. Regimental wives and their dependants would be required to lie low in the cellars of their German married quarters, bereft of any of the protective clothing and equipment issued to the troops for survival during a nuclear, biological or chemical onslaught. Stephen felt thankful to be single, and was briefly inclined to remain chaste.

The former Wehrmacht barracks occupied by the battalion were bordered on three sides by dark, towering forest. This perpendicular nether region was presided over by the local *Forstmeister*, a formidable figure distinctively dressed in a field grey outfit with green trimmings and invested with prodigious authority. Stephen could not recall any comparable phenomenon in the Forestry Commission back on the Salisbury Plain Training Area.

At the first officers' mess cocktail party organised by the CO to foster good relations with local German key personalities the *Forstmeister*'s daughter demanded to be introduced to Stephen. Gerda Schupp was still beautiful. Stephen was instantly struck by her angular symmetry and good command of English. She spoke freely about herself and her family, and she pre-empted any hesitation on his part to meet her again (she knew that bachelor officers were not allowed to entertain ladies in the mess) by mentioning that she lived in her own flat adjoining her parents' *Jagdschlösschen* on the northern edge of the forest. Stephen was listening with visible interest. The opportunity to shoot wild boar was not, however, at the forefront of Gerda's mind when she went on to invite him to dine at her parents' hunting lodge the following weekend.

In the meantime Stephen was sent on the first of a series of short courses run by the Royal Army Education Corps for prospective staff promotion candidates. His long-standing and leisurely interest in military history now deferred to the immediacy of war studies. Marxist-Leninist dogma was fomenting small-scale revolutions, insurgencies and acts of terrorism on four continents. While alarming to the Western world as a whole, these appeared to be psychologically absorbable by Stephen's adoptive country, with its long history of imperial conquest and pacification. The overarching threat of a so-called nuclear exchange between the two superpowers was an altogether different matter. Stephen's prescribed reading gave him his first exposure to two current concepts bordering on the unthinkable. The first of these was the prevailing idea among a few soaring political and military hawks that "mutual assured destruction", with its singularly apt acronym MAD, was actually a sound basis for strategic nuclear deterrence. The second was the less apocalyptic, and potentially more exploitable, notion that the Soviet Union both feared and fully expected a pre-emptive nuclear strike by NATO. Stephen could only imagine the implications of both scenarios for those living on either side of the Inner German Border.

XVI

Conversation at dinner with Gerda Schupp and her parents was conducted entirely in German. Stephen's early engagement with the English language had taught him the merit of achieving fluency in comprehension as well as in speech. He listened attentively as Herr Schupp described in detail the formidable array of qualifications needed to acquire a hunting licence in Germany, and he was relieved when the table talk started to revolve around less arcane topics, without once touching on politics. After three or four glasses of hock Stephen found himself conversing easily with Gerda and her father, unaware that Frau Schupp had for some time been watching him with maternally feral eyes.

Soon after the meal was over, Gerda resolutely led Stephen to her own wing of the house, while her parents formally wished him goodbye…until breakfast. He was left in no doubt about the extent of the Schupp family's hospitality, and he wondered whether there might be a tidy German compound word for what was being collectively encouraged between him and the *Forstmeister*'s daughter that night.

Gerda's lovemaking in the seclusion of her darkened pine bedroom was unconditional and passionate. When she finally loosened her embrace on her smitten and spent lover the tall trees outside her window were stirring uneasily in a strong wind which had suddenly swept down from the surrounding hills. Stephen lay back, elated, untroubled by wearisome guilt or remorse. Then he turned to face Gerda, and gently ran his fingers over the fine contours of her face before kissing her lightly on the forehead.

Stephen was awoken, some hours later, by the sound of suppressed sobbing. He sat up, and could just make out Gerda silhouetted against the window. She was sitting on the edge of the bed. Her square shoulders were tensely hunched and she was holding her head in her hands. Alarmed, he quickly moved to sit beside her. At first she would not let him touch her, and as the two sat together, naked and oddly vulnerable, she began to speak in tearful English. Stephen was unprepared for what he then heard.

'When war comes, West Germany will surely be overrun, even destroyed. I think your forces will not fight heftily for us. I am afraid. We watch here in Westphalia as your army trains for battle, moving westwards, always in the same direction.'

Stephen recognised the scenario for which he and his soldiers were currently training: a war of attrition which would see mechanised infantry and armoured divisions withdrawing from one line of defence to the next before, hopefully, delaying and destroying the Warsaw Pact armies on the River Weser; cold comfort indeed for a civilian population living between the Weser and the Elbe.

But how was he now to console this beautiful young German

woman who had somehow allowed an intense personal warmth to incubate a nationally conceived bête noire in the shared comfort of her own bed? He stood up, groped his way in the dark to the window seat, and retrieved his trousers. He had decided that this was not the moment to indulge in emotional fence-mending. He would engage her, rather, in gentle and measured conversation.

'Even though I've been here in Germany for only a few months, I do understand how you and many of your fellow countrymen must feel, Gerda. But you should be aware of two important things. In the first place, the German people will not be alone, if and when NATO forces go to war here. And secondly, an attacking Red Army can be defeated. Have you heard of the 1940 Winter War in Finland?'

'*Ja.*'

'Well then, you will know that the Soviet High Command has already had a taste of defeat at the hands of a much weaker but very much better motivated enemy.'

Once Stephen sensed that Gerda had calmed down, he changed tack.

'Tell me, Gerda, do you think that the Russians can count on the East German Volksarmee to fight kindred Germans this side of the Iron Curtain?'

'I think so...*ja.*'

'Are you sure? How about Soviet reliance on the Czechs, Hungarians and Poles?'

'I do not know, really. Perhaps there is hope for us.'

Gerda Schupp's visceral anxieties about the survival of her fatherland were temporarily suspended while she and Stephen carried on talking until daybreak.

Breakfast was a hearty affair. Gerda's parents were clearly satisfied with more than just the food on the table. By the time the emulous aromas of pickled herring and coffee had cleared, Herr Schupp was urging his daughter and Stephen to walk up to one of the firebreaks in the forest. There they could observe local game from a well sited and camouflaged hide.

While Stephen and Gerda were making their way along a narrow path through the evergreen gloom, wisps of cloud in the treetops indicated that they had already climbed some distance from the hunting lodge. As they rounded a bend where the path had just levelled out, a large pond came into view. The water was black and motionless, and there was no sound whatsoever to be heard. Stephen casually picked up a small, flattish pebble and sent it skimming across the surface. There was a sharp cry from close behind him, and he swung round to see Gerda's face briefly contorted in fear and fury. He instantly understood why. Hadn't Goethe himself written of dreadful retribution against those who wantonly disturb the tranquil but brooding forces of nature? Gerda said nothing, but her eyes warned Stephen of something hysterical and unforgiving. He and she never did reach the timber-frame hide in the firebreak. They retraced their steps down through the forest in silence.

Later that day, on his way back to the barracks, Stephen resolved to make light of his fractured relationship with Gerda Schupp. He surmised that few men of his fated ilk could claim to have been seduced by a young Teutonic woman so singularly passionate about war, and for whom a post-coital walk in the woods presaged some kind of supernatural ambush-in-waiting. From now on he would bide his time emotionally, in the hope of finding more manageable love or affection on his eventual return to England.

XVII

Stephen's regiment enjoyed a well-honed reputation for being "the thinking infantry". Discussion among Stephen and his colleagues in the comfort of the officers' mess was generally interesting and often animated.

In the weeks following his tactical withdrawal from the Schupp family Stephen was careful not to speak of his dissonant encounter with Gerda. In any case, he and two other young officers studying for the staff promotion exam had more important things to talk about.

After coming into the mess fresh from live anti-tank firing one afternoon, they started arguing about the dubious rationale of mutual assured destruction, unaware that the battalion second-in-command, a senior major of almost twice their age, was sitting quietly in a corner of the anteroom behind a newspaper. The conversation then turned to an idea which had particularly struck Stephen, namely that high-grade intelligence can be a significant "force multiplier". He understood perfectly the logic of using NATO brain to defeat Warsaw Pact brawn. And he sensed, not for the first time, his own potential role in all of this.

Having missed out on officer cadet training at Sandhurst, Stephen suspected that his career path would reach an early plateau. Besides, he was soldiering with brother officers of impressive military ability who were already destined for accelerated promotion. But he himself could, perhaps, excel through stealth, as it were. The dimly lit realm of intelligence-gathering and analysis now seemed to offer him an opportunity to fulfil a dawning ambition to serve his adoptive country with distinction. Ironically that was the one area in which any curiosity about his zealous patriotism could be his very undoing. This thought was just starting to nag him in rare moments of reflection between intensive training in the field and high spirits in the officers' mess.

One cold and fog-bound morning Stephen was summoned by the adjutant for an interview with the commanding officer. The CO, a tough, experienced and engagingly unorthodox soldier, greeted him congenially.

'Hello. Come on in and sit down a moment. I'll come straight to the point. While you and some of your sparkier brother officers are busy playing war games on all those staff promotion courses, I've got the job of maintaining a strong enough team to actually do the job. You're doing all right, and I propose to give you command of a rifle company within the next six months. But just now I'm faced with a dilemma. Someone in the Ministry of Defence wants to send you off on a long Russian language course. I've no doubt you'd do very well, given your academic background. But I have to tell you that this really isn't the time for you to throw up the chance of valuable command experience. So I intend to make a strong case for keeping you in the battalion for at least another couple of years.'

Stephen nodded gravely. He felt a brief pang of disappointment, but he knew that a further two or three years serving with his regiment would leave him free to soldier on with very little risk of untimely disclosure.

'I understand, Colonel. Thank you.'

The next three years passed swiftly for Stephen. Mechanised infantry training in Germany and Canada was punctuated by hectic four-month tours of duty in Northern Ireland. Despite seasonal riot control, an occasional brief firefight with inept terrorist gunmen and one narrow escape from a massive bomb explosion in West Belfast, he regarded the business of interposing himself between Unionist and Republican extremists as unedifying and irrelevant. He resented the loss of two of his youngest soldiers in shooting incidents six hundred miles west of the Iron Curtain. On the other hand, some of the more sinister aspects of counter-terrorism interested him. At one stage he was privy to some highly professional and unconventional covert operations being undertaken by others within his company's area of responsibility. He had no difficulty in overriding his contempt for a small number of key local informers whom he had personally recruited. And there was a shrouded compact between him and his close protection group in the event of cornering a lone IRA gunman.

Stephen had finally come of age in an era of blurred moral values, finely focused cynicism and universally failing religion.

XVIII

'Excuse me, sir. There's a telephone call for you from England.'

Stephen thanked the mess waiter, left the anteroom quickly and ensconced himself in the cramped phone booth just inside the front entrance.

'Hello? Who's speaking?'

'It's Melanie – Melanie Herring, you know! How are you doing?'

Stephen laughed, surprised to be hearing again from an old acquaintance with a shared interest in sidestepping family trees. They exchanged small talk for a while, before Melanie Sledge revealed that she was now working in London, "not a million miles from the Ministry of Defence". She went on to tell Stephen that she had heard that he was due to fly back from Germany for an interview in the MOD, and that she was looking forward to seeing him again. She gave him two contact telephone numbers. As soon as she had rung off, quite abruptly, a torrent of thoughts went running through Stephen's mind. How was it that he and this woman, with whom he had enjoyed only a passing friendship at university, were apparently still living and working in shadowy parallel? How did she know about a forthcoming interview which he had been told about by the adjutant only that morning? Who was she working for, and why her interest, and even involvement, in his army career?

He threw his old school scarf around his neck and strode out into the cold evening air for a brisk walk in the dark forest. There was a lingering smell of wood smoke, and he could hear wild boar grunting and rootling further up the hill. He was thinking more clearly now, and decided that he would accept Melanie Sledge's invitation to meet her in London. This time it would be his turn to lead with questions.

Five days later Stephen flew from Hanover to London and booked, under MOD arrangements, into a dismal hotel just off Piccadilly Circus. Even before unpacking his suitcase he telephoned one of the numbers given to him by Melanie Sledge. He recognised her cheery voice straight away.

'When's your interview in the MOD?'

'The day after tomorrow. I persuaded my CO to let me stay here for an extra day or two.'

'Good. I'll have a maroon cab pick you up outside the front entrance of your hotel tomorrow at 9am sharp. Just ask the driver to take you to Zephyrs.'

'But surely—'

'No problem, Steve. See you tomorrow.'

Young adults have a capacity for making good use of unexpected free time. Stephen flew down four flights of stairs to the hotel foyer, dropped off his room key at the reception desk and emerged breathlessly into Piccadilly Circus. He made straight for the Royal

Academy where he had heard that the Mellon Collection, spanning some two centuries of English art, was on display. As he wandered around this supremely national exhibition which had only been made possible through American wealth and patronage he became aware of a sallow girl eyeing him from a corner of one of the galleries. Within a few minutes the two enthusiasts were engaging in easy conversation and agreeing to have a late lunch together. The small restaurant which Stephen chose turned out to be exorbitantly expensive. They eventually parted without exchanging anything more than first names. Stephen shrugged resignedly as it dawned on him that his brief companion's admiration and passion had been only for fine arts and a free lunch. He then headed straight for Somerset House, home to the National General Register of births, marriages and deaths.

He was striding purposefully along the Victoria Embankment when he was met by a crocodile of supervised primary schoolchildren coming in the opposite direction. He smiled approvingly at the bright young faces, and caught sight of one of the older children, a sombre girl aged about ten, who was pulling a small boy along by the sleeve of his grey pullover. As soon as the chattering column had passed, he turned and glanced behind him. The dozen or so pairs of orderly children now all appeared to be holding hands. Stephen crossed the road to a stone balustrade and stared for a long time across the dark, swirling waters of the Thames.

When he finally reached Somerset House, the office that he planned to visit had just closed for the day. He returned, still on foot, to his cheerless hotel and went to bed without having had supper.

XIX

After devouring a full English breakfast, Stephen moved out to the front steps of the hotel at the appointed time and only had to wait for one minute before a maroon-coloured taxi drew up in front of him.

Stephen asked to be taken to Zephyrs, half-expecting the driver to say, 'Where's that?' But the man just nodded, and Stephen heard the click of an electronic catch being released on the nearside rear door. He climbed in and settled down for one of those entertaining conversations which are only to be had with a boisterously opinionated London cabby. When the driver seemed unwilling to chat Stephen turned his attention to the route the cab was taking. He was not familiar with Central London but still expected to spot a few well-known landmarks. Instead, he found himself being swept through a network of narrow streets whose names he either could not see or did not recognise.

When the cab finally came to a stop in a dark multi-storey car park the driver simply said, 'OK, sir, straight through that door,' and demanded no fare.

Stephen pushed open a grey steel door and found himself in

a stark, brightly lit corridor lined with ducts and cabling. He climbed a short flight of steps at the end of the passageway and pressed a promising-looking green button beside another steel door. After a short pause a disembodied voice on an intercom invited him to go on through. This time he was met by a drab middle-aged woman who escorted him to a lift and thence to a fourth-floor set of offices. All at once the atmosphere changed. Beyond an open office door sat Melanie Sledge, beaming at Stephen and telling him to close the door behind him. She was noticeably better groomed than in their Oxford University days, but she had lost none of her verve.

'Hi, Steve. Great to see you again. Well…very much the army officer now, eh? Let me make some coffee while you tell me a few of your war stories.'

She walked across to a bubbling percolator in the corner of the small office, and Stephen noted that not only was the room very sparsely furnished, but that there were no papers or files to be seen. A spiny cactus and a fleshy Venus flytrap adorned the windowsill.

He asked hesitantly, 'If it's not being rude, might I ask just where I am now, Melanie?'

'Well, Steve, you're in the office of a middle-ranking civil servant who hardly leads an adventurous life, but who rather likes men in uniform who do! How are things in Northern Ireland these days?'

'Pretty awful, and definitely not what I joined the army for.'

Melanie looked enquiringly at him and smiled. 'Here, have a coffee. So what did you join the army for?'

'Look. I don't want to sound too idealistic or high-minded, but I have a professional interest in preventing or preparing for a third world war, not tracking down armed hoodlums in the back streets of Belfast.'

Melanie nodded. 'Actually, it's interesting to talk to a serving soldier. How do you rate the Soviet Union's dependability on other Warsaw Pact armies in the event of war in Europe?'

Stephen was startled by her change of tack. 'How should I know?'

Melanie persisted. 'I should have thought that this was quite a hot topic in BAOR, or maybe you've had the opportunity to talk to a few West Germans about their "Easty" neighbours.'

Stephen answered, cautiously at first, 'We study all kinds of war scenarios as part of our preparation for the staff promotion exam which I sat last month. As for contact with Germans, my social life is pretty limited there. Needless to say, they see things very much from their own perspective. In fact I was recently on a joint field training exercise with the Bundeswehr, and the German divisional commander was openly critical of our own brigade staff who had been co-ordinating a phased withdrawal across reserved demolitions – you know, bridges ready to be blown and so on – while his own troops were conducting a series of assault river crossings due eastwards.'

Stephen checked himself. 'Sorry. I'm boring you.'

'Not at all. I find this all very interesting. Now tell me. This interview you're having in the MOD tomorrow – as you're going to the Main Building, presumably this heralds a promising career move for you?'

'I've no idea. I'm told that security vetting will probably be involved…and, well, I can say this to you, Melanie…it worries me a bit, you know.'

Melanie Sledge stood up, turned her back to him and, looking out of the window, said, 'My advice to you is just don't go further back than Stephen Yates.' She turned round to face him, leaned forward and said, 'Know what I mean? In any case, don't worry too much. You may be surprised how straightforward it turns out to be. Here, have some more coffee.'

Stephen felt no need for further reassurance. He leaned back, and was happy for his assertive Civil Service friend to continue leading the conversation, which she did.

'They tell me that military vetting officers are concerned less with politics and religion than with the three Bs.'

Stephen raised his eyebrows.

'Birds, bottles and boys.'

They both laughed together, but then Melanie looked him straight in the eye and said, 'By the way, I'm not one of your birds they should be remotely interested in, so perhaps you'd be good enough to make sure things stay that way.'

Stephen recalled some of their late-night conversations at university and assumed that she was referring to shared uneasiness about their respective Polish connections.

'Of course, I promise.'

Melanie smiled broadly. 'Great. Now, what have you been up to since we last met?'

They chatted amiably for almost an hour before Stephen eventually found himself being driven back to his hotel by another uncommunicative cab driver.

Once back in the hotel, Stephen reflected on his session with Melanie Sledge. The meeting had been distinctly one-sided. Having little else to do after a light supper in the hotel buffet restaurant, he went back to his room and began jotting down the salient points of Melanie's conversation with him. By reverting to her undergraduate persona she had deftly avoided disclosing anything about her work in the Civil Service. On the other hand she was now profitably au fait with many key aspects of his own professional and personal life. The British Intelligence and Security Services had a reputation for cloaking ruthless professionalism in geniality and charm.

XX

Some intrusive city sound awoke Stephen at six o'clock in the morning. He turned over and went to sleep again. When his alarm clock went off half an hour later he jerked awake in near panic. Confused and frenzied images from a slowly fading bad dream were rapidly overtaken by anxiety about his imminent interview at the Ministry of Defence. Only after an early hotel breakfast did he regain his composure.

The short walk to the MOD Main Building cleared his head and put him in a positive frame of mind. He would have felt more confident in uniform, but he was about to visit a government department where all servicemen were required to wear suits. He surmised that Oliver Cromwell, Lord Protector of the British Isles, had left an enduring legacy of suspicion and discomfort among civil servants. On arrival he felt overawed by the sheer size of the edifice in which he had an appointment. He was issued with a visitor's pass and then cast adrift in a Kafkaesque multi-storey labyrinth of lifts, staircases, "spines" and corridors. He arrived at the Intelligence Directorate office where he was to be interviewed with barely a minute to spare.

The unsmiling staff officer who invited him to take a seat introduced himself as Colonel Malcolm Swift and was clearly working under pressure. His desk was covered in files, and there was some embarrassed shuffling of paper before he felt able to launch into the interview.

'How's your French?'

'I speak good French, sir, and I think I could reach interpreter standard pretty quickly, if required.'

'All right. Now, you were probably expecting to be interviewed for a command or staff appointment out at Stanmore rather than here. However, this is not so much a career interview as a warning order. You have been selected for a posting to BRIXMIS soon after completing your Staff College course. What do you know about BRIXMIS?'

Stephen stalled. 'I haven't yet heard whether or not I've passed into the Staff College.'

'I can tell you now that you have, but this is strictly in confidence until the list of successful candidates has been published, all right? Now, how much do I have to explain to you about BRIXMIS?'

Stephen quickly overcame his elation at having achieved the most important step in his army career to date, and replied soberly, 'I have heard of it, since serving in Germany.'

Colonel Swift went on to give a thumbnail sketch of the British Commander-in-Chief's Mission to the Group of Soviet Forces of Occupation in Germany. The unwieldy title itself was misleading. An anachronistic Allied post-war liaison organisation drawn from the American, British, French and Soviet Armed Forces had actually evolved into a semi-covert and aggressive means of mutual intelligence-gathering on both sides of the Inner German Border. Stephen did not let on that he already knew this, and assured the colonel that he was more than happy to accept a grade two staff appointment in the mission, with special responsibility for liaison with its French counterpart, FMLM.

'Good. Now, I have in front of me the positive vetting questionnaire which you completed in Germany recently. Why, as a matter of interest, did you nominate an Oxford don as one of your two referees?'

'I thought he could probably give an unbiased assessment of my character and capabilities.'

Stephen was pleased with his own fluent response. Colonel Swift made no comment. Instead he ploughed through a prepared list of questions on Stephen's religious convictions, political affiliations, any visits to Communist countries during the previous ten years and, predictably, his views on drinking, women and homosexuality. Stephen's concise and unequivocal answers to each of these questions seemed to satisfy his hard-pressed interrogator, and the interview was suddenly over.

Stephen's account of his guileless security vetting quiz in the MOD amused Melanie Sledge when they met for lunch shortly before his departure for Germany. She insisted on paying the restaurant bill, even though this time she had found herself in the company of a somewhat more reticent old friend.

Lufthansa flights between London and Hanover were invariably comfortable and on time, despite a preoccupation with physical security shared only by the Israeli El Al airline in the early 1980s.

Stephen's regimental sword, which he had just collected after refurbishment in London and which he was carrying in his hand baggage, was hastily confiscated by a diligent and vexed cabin crew member who then served him a free drink. The passenger seated next to him made a jocular remark about an airliner being elegantly hijacked to Cuba, and then introduced himself as Alex Tisler, an electrical engineer living with his young family in West Berlin. He was, he explained, working with a number of other civilian technicians at RAF Gatow and was now en route to Hanover to pick up some equipment from a West German electronics firm. Tisler was about the same age as Stephen. As he chatted easily it transpired that he was of Czech parentage, without siblings and had been brought up and educated in Scotland. Stephen was asked nothing about his own family background, and for this he was thankful. Their in-flight rapport concluded with an invitation to Stephen to spend a few days sometime in Berlin with Alex Tisler and his wife, Kate.

Six weeks later Stephen had got permission from his CO to take five days' leave in the British sector of West Berlin. Armed with his Allied pass printed in French, English and Russian, he set off in his small car along the hundred-mile road corridor through East Germany to Berlin. This journey was calculated to be tense and unnerving. Individual drivers were carefully briefed by the Royal Military Police at Helmstedt on a whole raft of restrictions imposed to minimise the risk of an East-West incident: no stopping, no speeding, no deviation from the corridor, no photography…

Stephen's progress along the poorly maintained autobahn was uneventful, until he came over the crest of a long hill. A massive Soviet eight-wheeled armoured vehicle had collided with an East

German Trabant, a wretchedly fragile proletarian car built largely of pressed cardboard and synthetic resin. A pool of oil and blood was slowly spreading from beneath the crushed car, while the young crew of the BTR-60 were simply standing around looking unconcerned. No attempt was being made to extricate two people visible inside the wreckage. Stephen jumped out of his car, ran across to the Trabant and tugged hard at the driver's door, but could not move it. His gorge rose when he saw the damage inflicted on flesh and bone by over twenty tons of armour driven by an ill-trained and demoralised Russian conscript. The pulped bodies of the male driver and a woman with him had been fused together in a dreadful embrace. Both were clearly, and mercifully, dead. Then, below the sound of the wind, Stephen thought he heard a brief whimper coming from the back seat of the wreck. He leaned in through the broken rear window and saw that there was a child there. He gritted his teeth, grasped two very thin wrists and gave a long and painfully reluctant pull. But the wind was all that he had heard. He found himself rocking unsteadily on his feet, cradling the unmarked but lifeless body of a three or four-year-old. Her very frailty made him shiver.

The Soviet soldiers were still looking on sullenly and smoking when a Volkspolizei patrol car and a small recovery truck arrived. Some hasty orders were shouted in German. One of the policemen came up to Stephen and coldly relieved him of his harrowing little burden. Then, looking across at Stephen's car with its British Forces Germany number plates, he directed him to continue on his way without delay. As Stephen walked uneasily back to his car he saw the wrecked Trabant, with the two dead bodies still in it, being winched on to the recovery flatbed. He was witnessing for the first time morose dismissal of life in the German Democratic Republic.

He lost track of time for the last forty miles of his journey through the bleak, wintery landscape. Up to this day he had been untroubled by death, even violent death; he had always been able to distance himself from the victims, and had invariably been in the company of friends or fellow soldiers. This time it was different. Having been the only person at the scene to show concern, he now felt, paradoxically, that he had blood on his hands.

On arrival at the Dreilinden Allied Checkpoint in Berlin his irrational sense of guilt was compounded by his prompt arrest for taking thirty-five minutes more than the prescribed time to drive down the Berlin corridor. He spent the next three quarters of an hour making a detailed statement to an impassive sergeant of the Royal Military Police.

By the time he arrived at RAF Gatow Stephen felt drained of optimism and bonhomie. He was given an enthusiastic welcome by Alex and Kate Tisler and their small daughter, Katya. The child shook his hand politely, and stared at him while he closed his eyes for several seconds. She could not possibly have guessed what image he was trying to banish from his mind. Alex asked him if he was feeling all right, and he quickly pulled himself together.

XXI

Alex and Kate Tisler were pleasant and attentive hosts. Nothing was said about activities at RAF Gatow. But one afternoon an RAF Chipmunk training aircraft suddenly swooped low overhead.

'There goes BRIXMIS again,' said Alex with a grin. Stephen was surprised. He clearly had a lot to learn about that obscure organisation. But this could wait until later.

After a relaxing few days in Berlin Stephen drove back down the corridor, this time without incident, and returned to his battalion. Within six months he was on the move again. His attendance on a short course at the Royal Military College of Science, followed by a gruelling year at Staff College, Camberley, was a disagreeable but necessary career experience. He sometimes wondered who were more intent on scoring points, his aspiring fellow students or their frantically ambitious directing staff.

Having survived the ordeal, he was granted just enough leave to allow him to stay with his adoptive mother for a day or two, and also to visit the Standish family in Wilsford. There he found the old major alienated by dementia and his wife, Ethel, bitterly exhausted and depressed. She could only bring herself to speak of domestic trivia and mentioned, en passant, that the empty shell of the tortoise had been unearthed in the garden back in 1980. The hibernating creature was thought to have been eaten by rats.

One week later he found himself on an intensive course at the School of Service Intelligence in Kent. All the course students, bar a handful of American officers, were heading for a two or three-year tour of duty with BRIXMIS. They were briefed on the peculiar rules which governed intelligence-gathering operations, mutually agreed by the post-war Allies in Germany and euphemistically termed "liaison duties". No radios or personal weapons could be carried by any member of the military missions. Various means of circumventing these tedious restrictions were duly explained. For one hour every morning the students were shown fleeting shots of Soviet and East German military hardware which had to be correctly identified at a glance. Uncompromisingly high-grade photography was taught under the most testing conditions that could be simulated by the directing staff. Evasive "touring" techniques were practised out in the open countryside using a variety of souped-up vehicles. And the procedures to be adopted in the event of detention were thoroughly rehearsed. These included the prompt brewing of tea, to reassure their Stasi or Soviet captors that they were not about to make any reckless or violent moves. This greatly appealed to Stephen's painstakingly acquired sense of Britishness. The course concluded with the issue to students of a credible cover story to explain their activities in East Germany.

Within a week of reporting for duty with BRIXMIS Stephen

received an invitation to an al fresco supper party hosted by the general commanding the British forces in Berlin. He was seated with four couples who expressed a polite interest in his overt diplomatic liaison role vis-à-vis Group Soviet Forces Germany. The general, being an affable host, circulated among his guests, putting them at their ease. When he arrived at Stephen's table he bewildered him by introducing him as "one of our spies". Amid raised eyebrows and furtive smiles, Stephen was at a loss for words. He was not asked to elaborate, and as he thankfully tucked into his seafood cocktail he recalled that security consciousness in the British Army was, almost by tradition, inversely proportional to rank. In some perverse way, this might serve both to neutralise inquisitive listeners and to confuse hostile intelligence operatives. Stephen hoped so, anyway.

XXII

The next three years operating in the German Democratic Republic, albeit from a firm base in West Berlin, brought Stephen into constant and close contact with the Warsaw Pact "enemy". With nineteen Soviet and six East German divisions stationed in a country no bigger than Ireland, opportunities to observe military activity and equipment abounded.

Stephen felt entirely at home working from vehicles in dull matt green livery intriguingly modified to allow stealthy penetration into restricted areas, as well as unobtrusive photography and rapid escape from the ubiquitous Stasi, the East German Volkspolizei, the GDR Volksarmee and their grudgingly fraternal Soviet brothers-in-arms. He and his tour crew were deliberately rammed by a Soviet truck on only one occasion. A less fortunate French colleague was killed outright in a similar encounter.

One disgusting but highly productive source of information involved the retrieval of paper from latrines at the conclusion of major Soviet field training exercises. Stephen sometimes wished that Russian soldiers could be issued with toilet paper, so that they would not need to wipe their backsides on signals message pads and other documents of inestimable value to British Military Intelligence. Another even more revolting, and extremely dangerous, intelligence-gathering operation in the vicinity of a Soviet military hospital filled Stephen with such revulsion that he was thankful not to have to dwell on it. Inappropriately codenamed after a flowering shrub, it was so highly classified that it could hardly be spoken or written about within BRIXMIS, let alone outside.

The BRIXMIS Mission House, a lakeside former villa in Potsdam, was managed by an army warrant officer and his wife who took the occasional weekend off to go shopping in West Berlin. On these occasions other members of the mission were required to be on duty there, a generally uneventful and relaxing experience. Not so when it was Stephen's turn to man the place. It was a hot summer's day, and he decided to spend the afternoon tinkering with his bicycle outside the front entrance to the house. He noted, with some irritation, that the Stasi were photographing him from inside their Lada car parked outside the gate. Suddenly a young couple with two small children ran in through the gate and towards the house.

Stephen abandoned his oily task and intercepted them at the front door. They were in a state of great agitation and asked, in German, to be given political asylum. Stephen had to think on his feet. He knew that this was impossible under the terms of the 1944 Agreement, which established the peculiar status of both the Allied and Soviet military missions. He hastily explained to the now sobbing couple that they could only seek asylum through the British Embassy in East Berlin and that they must leave immediately. He watched, dismayed, as the hapless family was promptly detained by the Stasi waiting outside the gate and driven away to almost certain imprisonment.

A second Lada then drew up, with three men in it, and Stephen was summoned to speak with them. Being careful to stay a couple of feet inside the Mission House gate, he confronted the three "narks". An extraordinary conversation ensued which filled Stephen with alarm. His interlocutors addressed him by name and one of them smilingly explained, in fluent English, that the family who had just been arrested would not come to any harm and could be released without charge if Stephen would accompany them to their headquarters to make a statement. Stephen replied that this was out of the question, whereupon he was handed a letter. The Stasi promptly departed, leaving him to reflect gloomily on the plight of the ill-fated East German asylum seekers.

Only after he had contacted his headquarters at the stadium in West Berlin to report the incident did he open the letter he had been handed. His sense of anxiety intensified as he read its contents. Not only his army record of service but also his educational years and, most alarmingly, his childhood background were clearly known to the Stasi. He was invited to attend an informal meeting in the grounds of the Sans-Souci Palace *to discuss matters of mutual interest.* The originator of the letter must have been confident that it would not fall into the wrong hands, for Stephen promptly burned it in the garden of the Mission House. It then dawned on him that the episode involving the young East German family had probably been stage-managed to draw him away from both the security of the Mission House and the assurance of a promising military career.

Stephen's mind began to clear that evening as he gazed across the lake which divided the Mission House from an East German military museum on the opposite shore. Earlier positive vetting interviews had not probed his pre-Wilsford childhood. He had answered truthfully all the questions put to him and had so been security cleared to a high level. Now he had to decide whether to volunteer information about his Polish origin or to remain silent in the forlorn hope that his new Stasi acquaintances would not break that silence on his behalf.

Curiously, this decision was made for him three days later when he learned that the young East German asylum seekers had managed to reach the British Embassy in East Berlin and were shortly to be flown down one of the Berlin air corridors to West Germany. It seemed to him now that the Stasi approach might not have been elaborately contrived, after all. He would bide his time. His fierce loyalty to his adoptive country and to his regiment did not deserve to be cast in doubt by a security vetting organisation too easily blinded by chinks of light in an iron curtain.

XXIII

After two further years of piratical espionage with BRIXMIS Stephen returned to the UK for debriefings within the intelligence community.

At the so-called Government Communications Headquarters he was introduced to a number of men and women who were clearly of the same calibre as their World War II antecedents at Bletchley Park; brilliant linguists and outstanding intelligence analysts. The admiration was mutual. They listened intently to his every word. To them, he and his audacious colleagues were frontline operatives in an area with which they at Cheltenham were familiar through remote technology. They seemed particularly impressed with high definition, and sometimes breathtakingly close-up, photography of military hardware of which they had copious eavesdropped descriptors and electronic signatures, but perhaps only a partial visual image.

Interviews at Intelligence Directorates in the Ministry of Defence were brisk and straightforward. The staff officers concerned had already digested detailed reports of which Stephen had been either the originator or editor. He was complimented on the forced removal and theft of some highly classified equipment from Soviet command bunkers deep in the forests of East Germany. And there was unqualified praise for one of his colleagues who had single-handedly plotted an extensive network of unattended repeater stations, a landline system which would allow Group Soviet Forces Germany to launch a ground offensive across the Inner German Border in total radio silence. This threat was already causing GCHQ to lose sleep.

Stephen's final debriefing was in the building where he had last met his old friend, Melanie Sledge. This time it was another, and evidently more senior, member of her organisation who questioned him closely for over an hour on his access to human intelligence ("humint") in East Germany. He was asked what seemed to him to be a number of leading questions, but he avoided being drawn out on his encounter with the Stasi at the Mission House in Potsdam.

Nevertheless, he felt deeply uneasy as he went in search of the room in the next department to which he had been directed. This turned out to be the office of none other than Melanie Sledge. She greeted him with a broad smile, poured him coffee and seemed content for him to lead the conversation. It briefly occurred to him that she might have refined her interview techniques somewhat since they last met. Her friendly and relaxed approach put him at his ease, and he soon felt able to confide in her about the incident in Potsdam. She silently withdrew a thin file from a drawer in her desk and began to speak.

'I can well imagine why this has been troubling you, Steve. But you don't have to worry, old thing. The Easty family, as you know, made it safely to the West. So there's no suspicion here that they were part of a plan to compromise you.'

'But what about that letter the Stasi handed me?'

'Probably a coincidence. They may just have seized the opportunity to make an approach which had already been planned for some time. You sensibly destroyed it. End of story.'

Stephen felt his eyes filling with tears of relief at her professional reassurance and a certain tenderness dating back to their university days. She stood up, came round from behind her desk and kissed him fleetingly on the forehead.

'Dear Steve, you really have been through a tough time, haven't you? Your army career means so much to you, and I guess you understand well how my organisation works. In a hideously perverse way, patriotism and loyalty are seen as a potential liability rather than a priceless asset in people like you and me. We have something very special in common, Steve, and we must not let each other down. But promise me one thing. Should you ever be approached head-on by the Stasi or KGB, for God's sake come clean, not with me but with your boss at the time. Otherwise your whole life will unravel, believe you me. Promise?'

'Yes, Melanie, I promise. I'm just thankful that you and I have survived OK so far.'

After a good deal more coffee they parted company, closer friends than ever. Stephen had a spring in his step as he made his way to the shabby, and now familiar, MOD-sponsored hotel off Piccadilly Circus. This time his cheerless room enveloped him in a deep and untroubled sleep.

XXIV

As the Cold War progressed, albeit at a less menacing tempo, Stephen's life became increasingly subordinated to it. His next posting took him to a major headquarters in southern England. Here he worked in a staff branch responsible for UK operations and war planning. He felt comfortable and confident applying himself to the defence of his adoptive homeland. He was accorded a high security clearance, which gave him access to numerous key points. Among these were government and military underground installations sited and built to withstand nuclear attack. The decision to halt the expansion of one such secret location, on account of locally breeding natterjack toads, greatly appealed to Stephen's eagerly acquired British sense of humour. Later he dryly suggested at a security planning conference that Warsaw Pact defence attachés might have been tasked to introduce rare species at other KP construction sites. This caveat met with a stony silence, but was duly minuted.

Stephen spent much of his leisure time with a group of amateur archaeologists surveying and cataloguing ancient earthworks on the windswept grasslands of the Salisbury Plain Training Area.

They were occasionally joined by affable and quirky enthusiasts dedicated to protecting almost anything that grew or moved there. Among these was a stylish young woman called Lidia Morawska, a mycologist whose exotic name belied her unmistakable Englishness. Stephen did not share her interest in weird fungi, nor she his enthusiasm for archaeology. She nonetheless befriended him at every opportunity. She was hard-featured but pleasant enough, and he politely accepted her company during long strolls over the plain.

The United Kingdom Warning and Monitoring Organisation (UKWMO) managed an extensive network of small underground bunkers. These were to be manned by volunteers trained to record and report radiation levels in the aftermath of a strategic nuclear strike. There were a number of telltale grassy mounds on and around Salisbury Plain. Lidia Morawska showed more than a passing interest in these. She was soon asking Stephen searching questions about their purpose, and also about one much larger mound, with visible vents, which he knew to be the site of a top secret Regional Seat of Government. He had reservations about key politicians and civil servants in their concrete underworld being perhaps the only survivors of a thermonuclear war, but he was certainly not going to share his misgivings with Lidia Morawska, nor indeed discuss any KP matters with her.

Alarm bells began to ring with him, however, when she went on to quiz him about his role at Headquarters United Kingdom Land Forces. Could there be a husband somewhere who was even more interested than herself? Stephen by now felt too embarrassed to rebuff this persistent and plausible product of an elite West Country girls' boarding school. And so he reluctantly abandoned amateur archaeology, and devoted his free time, instead, to mastering the art of flying gliders at Upavon Airfield. He also took the opportunity to visit Tidworth Military Cemetery, where he found a surprising number of Polish war graves including no less than forty-one for the year 1947. Neither the Sikorski Military Museum nor the Polish Ex-Combatants Association in London seemed willing to supply further information on these burials. He mentioned this in a letter to his erstwhile language tutor at RAF North Luffenham. She replied a few weeks later, commenting that there had been an abnormally high suicide rate among Polish servicemen who had gone through the war. Stephen was left with an uneasy sense of something profoundly sad and wilfully unexplained.

Two years as second-in-command of a battalion in the Western Sovereign Base Area of Cyprus gave Stephen respite from unwelcome trespass on his professional and private life. He had no direct involvement in the East-West machinations which inevitably featured on an island of such strategic importance. He went along with the practice of asking no questions about the American U-2 spy plane which would take off in the early hours with a thunderous roar from RAF Akrotiri, but which was supposedly not based there at all. Russian "tourists" who regularly parked up in locked cars near various heavily guarded communications sites were someone else's problem. And when, as he drove past one particular aerial farm, two of the instrument needles on the dashboard of his car swung wildly before giving zero readings, he simply made a mental note to pay yet another visit to the local Volvo agent.

The Palestinian terrorist issue also impinged on Cyprus. Stephen was wary of one brief meeting set up with a member of Mossad. The Israeli Secret Service had an unmatched reputation for ruthlessness, and he idly wondered if this sinister outfit might have done its homework and was possibly even planning to recruit him into its ranks. There was no follow-up. Meanwhile windsurfing, sailing and seasonal snow skiing made his life easy and pleasurable.

Soon after his next posting back to the UK he was selected to go on a liaison visit to the Finnish Army. This brought him into contact with some intriguing personalities who seemed to merge effortlessly with their endless landscape of dark forests and myriad lakes. His phlegmatic hosts briefed him at length on the heroic Winter War against Soviet invaders in 1940; also on Finland's Paasikivi Doctrine of non-alignment and an impressive range of mobilisation plans for a future war against a diplomatically unspecified enemy. He felt curiously at ease in a country so unconnected with his own, and he relished the idea of tackling a language like none other, whose grammar boasted fifteen cases. So taken was Stephen with the Finnish culture and character that he decided he would apply for the post of defence attaché in Helsinki.

This opportunity presented itself two years later. He duly received his eagerly awaited posting order. But on opening the OHMS letter from the MOD he had to catch his breath. He was to be posted not to Helsinki, but to Warsaw. This bombshell raised a whole host of questions which reignited his deepest anxieties. Did it reflect a decision based on a full knowledge of his Polish birth and a plan to exploit this in some devious way? Or was it a fateful mischance which threatened to complicate his life immeasurably? Suddenly he felt a physical chill, and donned an old pullover, wincing as he noticed two holes in the cuff of his sleeve.

XXV

It was with deep misgiving that Stephen embarked on an intensive year of preparation for his appointment as assistant military attaché (technical) at the British Embassy in Warsaw. An informal meeting with his old friend, Melanie Sledge, had left him none the wiser about the reason for his posting to Poland. He knuckled down to several bewildering months of technical training at the Royal Military College of Science, and then the more familiar coursework at the School of Service Intelligence which had prepared him so thoroughly for BRIXMIS. Foreign Office briefings interested and amused him. One concise definition of diplomacy as the building of ladders for others to climb down particularly appealed to him as a soldier. The army had trained him to blow away an enemy on the top rung.

Then there was language training. The initial course in colloquial Polish in London was irksome. Stephen found himself closeted with a young Polish tutor in a windowless room for four hours a day. Her name was Katarzyna Wróblewska, and she seemed glamorously in denial of the Communist regime from which she had somehow absented herself. Elegantly dressed, she had an arrogant manner that Stephen found disagreeable, but she was a methodical teacher. He was careful not to reveal his early childhood acquaintance with the language. Within days he progressed from pointlessly simple phrases such as "*smutny pies*" (the sorrowful dog) and "*to jest kot, a to jest kotka*" (this is a tomcat but this is a she-cat) to more sophisticated grammar and syntax. Fluent conversation quickly followed. Katarzyna must have soon realised that he was contriving topics to suit his still limited vocabulary. One day she told him abruptly that from now on they would "play the truth game" ("*A teraz mówmy sobie prawdę*"). And so dialogue between them began to revolve around strictly factual information about their respective lives. Stephen responded well to this new initiative on her part, until she raised the subject of his imminent posting. She was clearly in no doubt about the dual role of a military attaché behind the Iron Curtain. He sensed danger. Small talk about cats and dogs had by now given way to discussion on Polish security restrictions and tips on how to talk one's way out of arrest. But one day a different conversational tack alarmed him very much more.

'*Znam pana siostrę.*' ("I know your sister.")

Stephen protested that he had no sister. But his tutor insisted that he had, and that she was unmarried, a former schoolteacher and youth leader now living in Warsaw. She would expect him to visit her there. He was utterly bewildered. Because the conversation had to be conducted only in Polish he was unable to phrase some of the questions to which he desperately needed answers. How could his tutor know about, let alone know, an alleged sister who was unknown to him? Was this revelation on a language course coincidental? Or was there some sinister plan behind it?

Katarzyna changed the subject for a while, but then returned repeatedly to it, finally passing Stephen a piece of paper with the Warsaw address and contact telephone number of Anna Śnieżko. He gazed at it and had to fight to hold back tears as the fading image of his childhood girl guardian revisited him for the first time in years. The colloquial language session concluded with a lengthy conversation about London theatre and Polish cuisine.

During the return train journey that afternoon, Stephen resolved to cast Cold War caution to the winds, and work tirelessly towards his three-year tour of duty in Poland. How could he possibly let slip this unique opportunity to decipher his lineage, his earliest memories; his very identity?

XXVI

Stephen was surprised when sent on an intensive Polish language course at an RAF station on Rutland Water; surprised, that is, by the signboard outside the course building which proclaimed it to be the Communications and Analysis Training School. It seemed extraordinary to him that a low-profile establishment set up to train intelligence-gatherers could have a title so certain to attract the attention of hostile foreign agents. But then he recalled that the Atomic Warfare Research Establishment at Aldermaston had recently been renamed the Atomic Warfare Establishment. Retaining the word "warfare" would surely guarantee, at the very least, continuing CND outrage and tiresome mass protest. Stephen surmised that there must be some subtle, and inimitably British, reason for denying deep cover to the nation's most secret installations.

His fellow students were talented young RAF corporals and sergeants who were already accomplished Russian linguists. Two of them had such pronounced Geordie accents that Stephen could only be sure of what they were saying once they had reached a fair standard of conversational Polish.

By contrast, their course tutor was an aristocratic Pole whose knowledge of English grammar and syntax was very much better than that of her NCO students. As the course progressed she began to reveal more about herself. Like so many of her wartime compatriots she had endured unspeakable suffering before finally arriving in England. Stephen's own half-remembered landfall had been untroubled by comparison. But his feeling of compassion and admiration for her was tempered by her outspoken bitterness against not only the Nazis and the Communists but also against the Jews. He felt deeply uneasy, and resolved to restrict conversation, in both Polish and English, to language-related topics. His strategy worked. He scored high marks in the Civil Service Polish Linguist Exam, and secured an invitation to keep in touch with his elegant language tutor after he had left North Luffenham.

Continuation training at the School of Service Intelligence gave a further boost to Stephen's morale. The work focused entirely on the Soviet Northern Group of Forces based in Poland. He would not, it seemed, be required to antagonise his Polish hosts by gathering a wealth of information on their own military equipment and war planning. This promised to make his professional and personal life much easier, once posted to the British Embassy in Warsaw.

And so, late in November 1988, Stephen found himself once again driving along the Berlin corridor through joyless and monochrome East Germany. This time he encountered driving snow but no luckless victims of DDR frigidity.

As an unmarried man Stephen was provided with a flat just a short distance from the embassy and so diplomatically observable.

The Warsaw he dimly recalled from early childhood was now no more. Post-war development under reluctantly embraced Communism had established a drab but secure enough way of life for most Poles. The capital, dominated by the monolithic Palace of Culture (Joseph Stalin's much-derided gift to the Polish people), was characterised by rigorous law and order, and by long queues for dull commodities in woefully short supply. Full employment appeared to prevail at very low cost to the state.

As one Polish mechanic at the embassy put it, 'They pretend to pay us. We pretend to work.'

Those who could afford them were driving around in bottom-of-the-market Fiats, tiny cars only marginally superior to their East German Trabant equivalents. A fractured and faulty communal central heating system was sending jets of steam through numerous cracks in the surface of the streets. Stephen was glad to have access to the small embassy shop and to a rate of exchange which would allow him to dine out without even thinking about the bill.

The Defence Section at the embassy operated in much the same way as BRIXMIS. Intelligence-gathering tours, however, had to be somewhat less piratical. Stephen and the highly trained senior NCO who accompanied him would be directly answerable to the ambassador for any entanglements with the Polish State Security Services. Diplomatic immunity came at a price.

Domestic and social life in Cold War Warsaw promised to be void unless Stephen could find something other than the embassy piano for company. And so his eye was caught by a tall, dark-haired young clerical assistant working in the Political Section. Olive-skinned Erica Mendel had generous features and an easy smile. After one particularly gruelling three-day tour of Soviet training areas Stephen decided to take the plunge and ask Erica to dine out with him. She beamed with pleasure, but then a strange shadow fell across her face. She hesitated for a moment, and only then agreed to be taken out to a fashionable restaurant beneath the streets of Warsaw's Old Town. Stephen was already beginning to feel a strong affection for his professional colleague, and resolved to make her feel special.

The very next day Stephen's thoughts turned to another, and potentially more fraught, relationship. Up to now he had repeatedly put off the decision to visit the address given to him by Katarzyna Wróblewska. The opportunity to finally meet the most important person in his early life could be delayed no longer. He had already found the street, Ulica Wałbrzyska, on his Warsaw city map. He agonised over the wording of a letter, in Polish, to Anna Śnieżko. He made no allusion to their possible kinship, simply quoting Katarzyna Wróblewska as a mutual acquaintance. Professionally instilled caution had long taught him to share information on a strictly need-to-know basis. The onus would be on this alienated woman to reveal her, and perhaps even his, true identity.

He winced involuntarily when he eventually pushed the letter into a shabby local postbox. Had not Pandora visited terrible afflictions upon men who pried into women's secrets?

XXVII

Erica Mendel was oddly silent as Stephen drove her to the Old Town for their first evening out together. His diplomatic registration plates allowed him to park close to the exclusive cellar restaurant frequented by senior politicians, diplomats and prominent intellectuals. Stephen had already enjoyed some affordable evenings there in noteworthy company. On this occasion the head waiter who met them at the foot of the downward winding staircase gave Stephen a familiar nod but then fixed Erica with an icy glare. There was a moment's hesitation before they were shown to a table behind a brick pillar in an ill-lit corner of the restaurant.

After an unreasonably long delay a waitress, whom Stephen recognised from a previous visit, appeared. His few friendly words in Polish were greeted with silence. This unpromising start set the tone for an evening of discourtesy and slow service. Stephen and his new friend ate well enough but struggled to chat cheerfully about diplomatic life in Warsaw. He realised what was wrong. Erica had been instantly recognised as Jewish, and probably not for the first time when out in the city. He knew that anti-Semitism was still prevalent in Poland, but was nevertheless shocked to encounter it first-hand. They finally left without having had coffee.

By the time they reached her apartment she was weeping quietly. Stephen squeezed her hand gently as he wished her goodnight, and watched with a heavy heart as she disappeared through her front door. On the way back to his own flat he pondered gloomily on that timeless affliction, shared unequally with Erica Mendel, from which there was, of course, no escape.

Stephen slept soundly that night, and by the following morning was looking forward to more intelligence-gathering tours which would put him in a healthier frame of mind. However, in advance of a clutch of visits by VIPs from the UK the defence attaché asked him to reconnoitre not only military installations but also various places of key historical interest. And so Stephen found himself over the following three weeks visiting the sites of some of the Third Reich's most infamous extermination camps in Poland.

The first fact that struck him was the very names of these places: Brzezinka (Birkenau), "Little Birch Wood", where Himmler's gas chambers had operated around the clock to rid Auschwitz of its countless unproductive prisoners; Majdanek, "Small Woodland Glade", where a gigantic concrete cupola now covered the ashes of eighteen thousand inmates who had been killed in a single day, to the sound of music played over loudspeakers to drown the sound of shooting and the cries of the dying; Gross Rosen, "Abundant Roses", where a wrought-iron crown of thorns now adorned the only remaining crematorium chimney. Then there was Treblinka. How prettily the name tripped off the tongue. Yet it was there that ninety-nine per cent of the camp's nine hundred thousand prisoners had been put to death within three hours of arrival at the railway offloading point. The enormity of the crimes committed against Jews at these dreadful places made Erica Mendel's wounding encounter at the Świętoszek Restaurant seem like a mild rebuff.

XXVIII

On returning to his flat after a short spell of local leave, Stephen was surprised to find that the Polish security services, the SB, had paid an unannounced visit. His deep-freeze cabinet had been unplugged from its wall socket and smelled of rotten meat. Some of his books had been rearranged on their shelves, and blobs of strawberry jam had been dropped across the parquet flooring. He had heard of similar calling cards being left by the Stasi in East Germany, but was disappointed that his Polish hosts were resorting to the same kind of low-key harassment. However, his irritation was quickly forgotten when he spotted a letter on the inside front doormat. It bore the name of Anna Śnieżko.

Stephen poured himself a stiff drink and sat down to read the long-awaited letter. It was four pages long and, surprisingly, was written in regular italic handwriting. It described in passable English how she had brought her small brother to England in late 1942 and left him with the British Red Cross. She had then returned to Poland, via Sweden, only to be imprisoned by the Nazis for black-marketeering. She went on to recount a hard life growing up and finding work in post-war Poland. Her letter ended by inviting Stephen to visit her at her home the following week, and concluded with the words *Your loving sister*. Stephen wept, at first with emotion but then with frustration at so many unanswered questions. Why had she returned to Poland in 1943? Why had she apparently then made no effort to make contact with her young brother? And why, eventually, through his first language tutor, Katarzyna Wróblewska?

As the day for their first meeting approached Stephen became increasingly apprehensive. His English upbringing had taught him to keep a tight rein on his feelings, but now he was facing the greatest emotional upset of his life. Perhaps as a subconscious hedge against disappointment he suddenly felt the urge to be with Erica Mendel again. He called in at her office in the embassy, and secured an invitation to her apartment the following evening.

Erica cooked Stephen a tasty kosher meal and they listened to music on her stereo player while they sipped coffee. They chatted long into the night. Each avoided talking shop, knowing that the room was probably bugged.

Suddenly she said, 'There's something troubling you, isn't there?' And she unexpectedly gave him the tenderest kiss he could recall.

As she drew back a little, with the easy smile which by now so attracted him, he just whispered, 'Thank you, dear Erica', and left.

XXIX

Stephen suffered a feverish night on the eve of his first encounter with Anna Śnieżko. Against his better judgement he had descended into emotional turmoil. What would it be like to meet his own flesh and blood after so many years as a displaced kinsman? Would she attach any value to those fragmentary childhood memories which were still so precious to him? Could he and she possibly by now feel mutual affection? Would there be an agonising language barrier? And what of her true identity? Would she admit to being Jewish, or else a Catholic convert of convenience? Or would she simply turn out to be the soulless product of some four decades of Communist indoctrination? When he finally awoke to a grey dawn, Stephen dreaded what might lie ahead of him that day.

Ulica Wałbrzyska was not difficult to find. He quickly spotted the house number he was looking for and drew up outside. He sat in his car for several minutes, feeling sick with apprehension. He glanced up to see a face peering expectantly through one of the front windows of the drab house. Before he was able to knock on the peeling door it was opened, and he found himself face to face with the only person in the world who might now shed light on his earliest years; who might somehow repossess him.

Anna Śnieżko was dressed entirely in grey. She opened her arms wide and embraced Stephen fleetingly.

She then took a step backwards, smiled broadly, and said in heavily accented English, 'So, my little brother. How long we have not met!'

Her words left Stephen unable to speak, or even think, clearly. He suddenly realised how ill prepared he was for this moment.

The house was very cold. Anna carried on in fluent, if somewhat imperfect, English. She explained that they would now sit down to coffee and cake and talk about the past. And so it was, giving Stephen the chance to look long and hard at this strange sibling. She was slightly built and rather shorter than him. Her close-cropped straight hair showed little sign of greying, and her strikingly blue eyes moved constantly from side to side as she spoke. Stephen found this disconcerting, but resolved to look at her unflinchingly, in an effort to build up some kind of rapport. He had in his mind a fixed image of the anonymous girl who had brought him from Poland to a new life in England in 1942. Now he struggled to see this likeness, or even a vestige of it, in Anna.

As she talked on, however, the shadows of the past began to shorten. During the course of their conversation, which continued for a full two hours, she touched on a number of shared memories, unprompted and in a curiously detached way. She recalled the train journey from Zamość to Warsaw, the safe house in Podbipięty, the onward rail journey to Danzig, the long sea crossing to England, but made no mention of the host family in Wilsford. She went on to describe how she had been repatriated to German-occupied Poland with the reverse help of Żegota, and how she was soon afterwards sent to Auschwitz, having been caught black-marketeering in the Łódź ghetto. At one point she rolled up her left sleeve and showed Stephen a number unevenly tattooed on her forearm. He was close to tears, and failed to memorise that fateful number. She went on to describe a life of hardship in post-war Poland. Stephen noted that she never once spoke ill of the Communist Party which had presided over her probable deprivation, both material and cerebral.

Having recovered his composure, Stephen began to question his sibling about things which he felt must be of intense mutual concern.

'What happened to our parents?'

'Your father died fighting in the area of Bydgoszcz. Mother was killed during an air raid on Warsaw.'

'How did you survive Auschwitz?'

'I was useful to the camp staff as a calligrapher. I was still quite fit when the Russians liberated us.'

'How did you manage, as a Jew in Poland, after the war?'

'I never looked Jewish. I wore long sleeves, worked as a junior school teacher and youth leader, and I went to church often, like you did.'

'How do you know that?'

'My friend, Katarzyna, has told me.'

Stephen remembered his glamorous colloquial language tutor in London, and wondered how much other information about him she might have gleaned during those claustrophobic Polish conversation sessions.

His attention quickly returned to Anna. He noticed that her eyes were now moving less frequently. As she began to discuss when they might meet again, Stephen found himself held by her steady gaze, and he suddenly felt a strong physical attraction, which disturbed him. Surely this was an unnatural feeling for a sister? But then how, as a virtual only child, could he possibly know about such things? He felt flushed and uneasy when he stood up to leave, having decided on a mutually agreed date for their next meeting. She opened the front door and stood there for a moment, her chin raised, her eyes closed, poised for an inescapable kiss on her cracked lips.

Stephen had two near collisions in the Warsaw rush-hour traffic as he drove back to his familiar digs.

XXX

There was some urgent intelligence-gathering to be done the following week. The Ministry of Defence in London had been alerted to a series of trains with Soviet military equipment heading west towards East Germany. The MOD needed to know whether this signified a major re-equipment programme for Group Soviet Forces Germany, or else a large-scale deployment exercise, possibly as a precursor to a ground offensive across the Inner German Border.

Stephen and his accompanying senior NCO hastily packed camera film and emergency rations into their tour car and drove out into the wintery countryside. For six days and nights they observed and photographed "kit" trains from reconnoitred hides on main lines running through densely forested areas of Western Poland. Nearly all the military hardware which rumbled past them was tarpaulined, but this did not prevent the two rigorously trained men from identifying one of the latest Soviet ground-to-air missile systems, as well as some three hundred of the latest T-80 tanks fitted with explosive reactive armour.

One evening they had to pull back quietly into the forest when a kit train unexpectedly screeched to a halt directly in front of them. To their surprise half a dozen Soviet soldiers jumped down from a covered freight wagon, squatted down and defecated beside the railway line. After a few minutes two loud whistle blasts came from the colossal steam locomotive. The soldiers clambered back on board, and the train went slowly on its way into the gathering darkness. A little later that night Stephen reverted to his BRIXMIS mode, pulled on a pair of rubber gloves and hastily picked up sheets of soiled Soviet newspaper and signals message pads, as well as defiled pages from what would later turn out to be a training handbook for operators of electronic warfare equipment.

A Foreign Office telegram received at the embassy the following week indicated that technical intelligence analysts at the Ministry of Defence in London were little short of euphoric over the photo-imagery and intelligence-yielding filth gathered by Stephen. And there would have been relief in London that what was being witnessed in Poland was a major equipment upgrade of Group Soviet Forces Germany and not the overture to a Soviet all-out attack on NATO.

Stephen felt elated; all the more so when summoned to report in person to the ambassador's office. The ambassador invited him to take a seat and then, while glancing from time to time at a file on his desk, complimented him on a job exceptionally well done. He added that he also appreciated how the Defence Section had managed to carry out aggressive intelligence-gathering without running into the kind of trouble which would put him, the ambassador, in a difficult diplomatic position vis-à-vis the Polish Defence Ministry.

Stephen was in a buoyant mood as he walked out through the adjoining office of the Head of Chancery. He had long harboured a desire for recognition of loyal and focused service to his adoptive country. He knew that this latest intelligence coup, endorsed by a senior diplomat, might even make him eligible for a civil or military decoration. Most of his army contemporaries would probably think little of having an MBE added to a chestful of hard-won campaign medals. But to Stephen an award of this kind would represent something hitherto unthinkable: acceptance into a quaint order of chivalry which his lineage alone should have put well beyond his reach in an unending Cold War.

XXXI

During those interminable rail watches in the snowbound forests two hundred miles west of Warsaw, Stephen had had plenty of time to think about his first encounter with Anna Śnieżko.

On the agreed date of their second meeting he arrived at her house better prepared for a session which he hoped would start to build up mutual trust between them. He was irritated, therefore, by her obvious determination to lead the conversation. She began by speaking about her various teaching jobs and her work with boy and girl scouts. But then she abruptly turned to Stephen's military background and his attaché role at the British Embassy.

In an effort to satisfy her curiosity he reminisced briefly about his life as an infantry officer. He then went on to tell her about official liaison with the Polish Armed Forces and responsibility for the care of the three British war cemeteries in Poland. He also spoke of occasional meetings with Polish ex-fighter pilots who had distinguished themselves during wartime service with the RAF. At her insistence he touched on the modus operandi of Defence Section tourers. But he took pains to assure her that they had no quarrel with their host nation, and that they always steered clear of Polish military installations.

This prompted her to ask, 'So you are more interested in the Soviet forces here in Poland?'

Stephen sensed danger, and chose his words carefully.

'We operate within the strict rules applied to military attachés the world over. We are identified by diplomatic number plates on our vehicles, and we respect Polish laws and traffic regulations.'

'No weapons or radios?'

'Absolutely not.'

'Poland is a big country. How do you know where to go to do your work?'

Stephen suspected that she was angling for information on the Defence Section's intelligence sources. Highly classified links with GCHQ, MI6 and BRIXMIS were rarely, if ever, discussed openly within the embassy, let alone with outsiders, and categorically not with Polish nationals. He quickly changed the subject.

'Tell me, Anna, do you and I have other brothers and sisters?'

'No.'

'When you brought me to England during the war, didn't you think that we should stay together?'

'That would have been nice, yes. But Żegota needed me to help get other Jewish children out of Poland.'

'But you didn't even contact me for all of forty years. Why not?'

'I am really sorry, you know. But our Communist authorities would not allow close links with relatives living in the West.'

'And yet you now feel free to renew our kinship, our friendship, even. So what's changed?'

'Much has changed in the last few years. You may not understand how. Have more coffee.'

By now Stephen was beginning to suspect that his sister had some kind of alter ego or hidden agenda – or however the English language might deftly describe duplicity on her part. He had some more leading questions to put to her, but these could wait until their next meeting. They agreed on a date in the very near future.

XXXII

Stephen was impatient to see Anna Śnieżko again, and so he was exasperated at having to postpone their next meeting indefinitely. Both the Embassy Cultural Section and the British Council in Warsaw were too busy to host a historian from Hull University conducting research into the Holocaust. Stephen was given the job of escorting the visitor to Auschwitz. During the long and tedious drive south he gave Professor Mark Lipmann a well-informed briefing on the Nazis' systematic pursuit of the Final Solution in German-occupied Poland.

They arrived at Auschwitz late that morning and parked up alongside four German tourist coaches. The camp was grimly familiar to Stephen. However, he spotted a new sign just inside the infamous *Arbeit Macht Frei* main gate, which showed that a new photographic exhibition had been set up since his previous visit. His guest spoke quietly into a miniature tape recorder as they worked their way around the various sickening displays in the former prisoners' accommodation blocks.

When they arrived at the recently assembled collection of

photographs, which occupied the entire floor of one building, they split up. Mark Lipmann appeared to be interested in imagery covering the rail transport system which had linked Auschwitz with Jewish ghettos and the other concentration camps. Stephen was drawn towards countless sets of identity photographs which had been taken of all new arrivals at the camp. Each prisoner had been photographed in three separate poses: one in profile, one face-on and one at an angle wearing either personal or camp headgear. All of the men and some of the women had shaven heads. Very few looked defiant. Most were expressionless, seemingly resigned to their fate. Many were little more than children. Stephen sighed deeply as he walked at an even pace, as if reviewing a parade of the damned.

Suddenly he froze, rooted to the spot. He was looking straight into the eyes of the girl who had brought him out of Poland so long ago. The darkish hair cut straight above the nape of her slender neck and pinned back with a kirby grip; the thin face framing deep-set dark eyes; the distinctive mouth with a slightly protruding lower lip; the knowing look which had so grown on him as an infant; all these features sprang out at him from that woeful little triptych. With his head swimming he lowered his gaze in an effort to efface those three images. But when he looked up again there was no shadow of doubt that this was his svelte and sombre childhood guardian.

Now he focused on the factual information on the photograph in profile. He noted the young prisoner's five-figure camp identification number; also her ethnic descriptor, of which only the last three letters were visible on the cropped photograph.

At that moment Mark Lipmann reappeared, looked hard at

Stephen and asked him if he was feeling all right. Stephen blew his nose, drew himself up soldier-style and briskly outlined his plan for the rest of the day. They would take lunch in the visitors' canteen, lay an embassy wreath at the Execution Wall, and then drive to nearby Birkenau with its railhead, prisoners' huts, gas chambers and crematoria in varying degrees of preservation.

Lunch in the canteen was a miserable experience for both men; though not, apparently, for a noisy party of elderly West Germans who were enjoying an animated discussion about their home town of Wuppertal. The soup was thin, greasy and lukewarm. The rye bread was stale, and the only choice of main course would also have been darkly reminiscent of concentration camp rations, had it not been proclaimed on the menu card as *bigos*, a dubious stew still popular with most Poles.

Stephen was an indifferent guide that afternoon. His mind was no longer on the systems and statistics which interested his guest.

It was dark, and snowing hard, when they finally arrived back in Warsaw. Before being dropped off at his hotel Professor Lipmann presented Stephen with a signed copy of his recently published analysis of the meticulous records maintained by none other than the perpetrators of the Holocaust in Europe.

Once back in his flat, Stephen heated up some food, downed half a bottle of red wine and began brooding over the day's events. His emotions were in turmoil. Then his intelligence training kicked in, and he calmly weighed up the facts he had gleaned from the camp identity photographs of his sister. His sister? He now began to wonder. Would the young prisoner's serial number on the photograph correspond with the number tattooed on Anna Śnieżko's forearm? He would soon be finding out.

In the meantime there was something else to be considered. The last three letters of the ethnic descriptor on the cropped photograph were, he remembered, *–ole*. Every Jewish prisoner's mugshot had been labelled with the German word *Jude*. Most non-Jews had been described by their nationality. The letters *–ole* could mean only one thing. The young girl in the photograph had been classified by her Nazi captors as a non-Jewish Pole. Stephen's thoughts turned again to Anna Śnieżko. Had she really been able to conceal her Jewishness in the face of German ethno-scrutiny?

Stephen suddenly felt drained of energy. He poured himself another glass of wine and started to dip idly into the book he had been given. It was well indexed, and he was roaming from one topic to another when he was abruptly reminded of a fact which he had hitherto overlooked. Only from the winter of 1940 to early 1943 were Auschwitz inmates photographed in three poses. Thereafter, those identity photographs were replaced by numbers tattooed on the left forearm. Stephen was wide awake again. Here was both an ethnic and a chronological mismatch between his sister and the unmistakable young girl in the Auschwitz photographs. Anna Śnieżko would now have to convince him that she was who she claimed to be.

That night Stephen was revisited by the strange chalk pit nightmare which had last troubled him during his earliest childhood days in Wilsford.

XXXIII

The following morning Stephen was unexpectedly told by the defence attaché that he was free to take one week's leave. He immediately telephoned Anna Śnieżko, and arranged to meet her, once again at her house, the very next day.

He would have liked to enlist the kindly support of his friend, Erica Mendel, in preparing himself for what promised to be a crucial meeting. However, he was told that she would be working until late that evening on urgent business at the embassy. So he returned to his flat, and set about marshalling his thoughts and drawing up a list of questions which he would put to his putative sister. He also drafted two letters, one to the Auschwitz-Birkenau State Museum; the other to Yad Vashem, the Holocaust Martyrs' and Heroes' Remembrance Authority in Jerusalem, requesting information on the unidentified young female prisoner. He quoted her camp identity number and asked, among other things, for her name, age in 1943 and date of death. He requested, too, details of the former prisoner Anna Śnieżko, convinced by now that his enquiry related to two separate people.

On the day of his third meeting with Anna, Stephen was braced for a chilling encounter. Her house was extremely well heated on this occasion. This paradox served one useful purpose. Her sleeves were rolled up, revealing her tattooed camp identity number. This time he took care to memorise it. It was not the same number as that which he had noted at Auschwitz. From that moment the conversation over coffee and cake was steered in the direction already planned by Stephen.

'Do you remember much about our sea crossing to England back in 1942?'

'Not really. All ships are the same to me. I do not like the sea.'

'Were we able to take any special possessions with us?'

'No, just our clothes. I suppose you had one or two toys.'

'When you finally left me with the Red Cross in England, where then did you go?'

'Back to Poland. You know that.'

'When we last met you asked me a lot of questions about my role here as an attaché.'

'I was interested. I did not know anything at all about military attaché work.'

Stephen detected Anna's growing unease, and stopped short of questioning her about her time in Auschwitz. When he finally left through the front door he was treated to an exaggerated show of sisterly affection, which he grudgingly reciprocated.

On returning to his flat he redrafted his letters of enquiry to Oświęcim and Jerusalem to include the Auschwitz camp identity number of Anna Śnieżko.

Stephen spent the rest of his leave exploring Warsaw by car and on foot. He scoured bookshops for up-to-date tourist maps of areas in which several intelligence directorates at the MOD had expressed an interest. He was not surprised to see that all military barracks, training areas and airfields had been studiously omitted by paranoid state mapmakers. Nevertheless he knew that these travel maps might usefully complement or confirm imperfect satellite photo-imagery.

On three evenings he dined out, alone, at restaurants recommended by embassy colleagues. He spent his final Saturday with Erica Mendel. That afternoon they sat, warmly wrapped up against the cold, for almost two hours on a concrete bench in the Saski Gardens. There, with no risk of being overheard, they talked about Stephen's increasingly fraught relationship with Anna Śnieżko. He had hoped that Erica might offer some professional, measured advice. Instead she simply urged him to "ditch" the woman who was clearly a fraud. He quickly realised that sound judgement had been overtaken by jealousy of a perceived Jewish rival.

Once they were back at Erica's flat she offered him very little to drink but treated him to another wholesome kosher meal. With little of interest to talk about in the presence of probable bugging devices, they retired early to bed – Erica's bed. Breakfast the next morning was something of a celebration for Erica Mendel.

XXXIV

Over the previous three years Stephen had been required to obtain periodic water samples in the vicinity of Soviet thermonuclear weapons storage sites in central Poland. He was not privy to the exact purpose of this mundane exercise, codenamed Operation Minos. But he knew that it had something to do with measurable levels of tritium, a radioactive isotope of hydrogen. Then he had been tasked by the Ministry of Defence in London to collect samples of water and soil from inside a nuclear storage site recently vacated by the Soviets. Suspecting that scant heed would have been paid to decontamination by the departing tenants, Stephen and his touring colleague had decided to make this a quick in-and-out job. Unluckily for them, they had been forced to hide inside one of the bunkers for almost an hour while a chattering family pottered around gathering edible fungi just outside the perimeter fence.

When Stephen went to collect his mail from the embassy on his return from leave he was shown a signal from the MOD which acknowledged receipt of his latest mineral samples and ordered the immediate cessation of Operation Minos.

Over the next two weeks Stephen was, at his own request, taken off touring duties while he contended with periodic dizziness and vomiting. He stopped eating out. Then he received replies to both his recent letters of enquiry. Yad Vashem regretted that they could not disclose information relating to concentration camp identity numbers alone. The letter from the Auschwitz-Birkenau State Museum was more informative, and utterly perplexing. It confirmed that the young Polish girl in the trio of photographs was born in 1928, sent to Auschwitz in April 1943, liberated in early 1945 and died in 1980, and that her name was Anna Śnieżko. The other camp identity number quoted by Stephen had been allocated to a Polish Jew called Zofia Plucik.

As he stared at the letter, the enormity of the deception inflicted on him left Stephen breathless and numbed for some ten minutes. He resisted the temptation to have a stiff drink, and settled down to make some sense of this personal perfect storm. To rebuild his battered selfhood he would first have to deconstruct his spurious sister. This would not be difficult. Zofia Plucik, as she now was, had failed to recall those very details of Stephen's accompanied journey to England in 1942 which would surely have been unforgettable to her: the extraordinary submarine voyage from Denmark, wartime life with the eccentric host family in Wiltshire, an important stop-off in London before returning to Poland, and then there was the tortoise. How could she possibly have forgotten her other small charge during that wartime odyssey? Stephen smiled ruefully to himself as he pondered on the irony of that somnolent creature alerting him, after all these years, to a grotesque betrayal of trust.

Stephen's thoughts now turned to the real Anna Śnieżko. And

with those thoughts came an unstemmable flood of emotions. Here was the person who, at the tender age of fourteen, had saved his life. And yet it was not what she was, but what she was not, that overwhelmed him. She was not Jewish, so could not have been his sister. She was not Jewish, and yet had risked everything to protect some stranger's child destined to become untimely, worthless ash. She was not Jewish, and would have been well received in respectable rural England, but had chosen, instead, to return to German-occupied Poland – perhaps to help another doomed child to escape? Momentarily shedding his now middle-aged sangfroid, Stephen wept bitterly, and silently forgave her for not trying to contact him after the war. Why should she? She had endured two years in the very death camp which had almost certainly awaited him. She would have needed immeasurable oblivion and renewed courage to rebuild her broken life. Strange that she should finally have died in the same year as her familiar childhood tortoise.

Several days passed before Stephen began to think again about the elusive Zofia Plucik. He felt a physical chill as the implications of his contact with her began to dawn on him. She was a dissembler who had shown an abnormal interest in his work as an attaché. If his relationship with her were to come to the attention of his military masters he would be declared a major security risk and his army career would be effectively ended. But then he thought back to his encounter with the Stasi at the BRIXMIS Mission House in Potsdam, and to Melanie Sledge's reassurance that the incident had passed below the MOD security radar. But there again, it was his civil servant friend who had also warned him to report immediately any further unsolicited approach by Eastern Bloc nationals. With his thoughts in disarray, he finally fell into bed. That night he dreamed again of the bramble-filled chalk pit, but this time set in the surroundings of Auschwitz-Birkenau. When he awoke the following morning he was aware that he had still not shaken off whatever bug was causing him to feel unwell.

XXXV

Stephen's next tour of Soviet training areas ended successfully with the recovery of depleted uranium ammunition from an anti-tank range. But any elation on his part was tempered by his decision to report his encounters with Zofia Plucik to higher authority. His next debriefing at the Ministry of Defence in London would provide the ideal opportunity to do this, sparing him the embarrassment of confronting his defence attaché at the embassy.

Three days later he found himself ensconced once more in the grim MOD-approved hotel just off Piccadilly Circus. From there he immediately telephoned Melanie Sledge. He was given a new telephone number by the operator and was soon chatting to his old friend. They arranged to meet the next morning.

The procedure for visiting Melanie at her place of work was by now familiar to him. He was amazed, however, to recognise the anonymous cab driver who had driven him there some ten years earlier. The recognition was mutual.

'You all right, sir?'

'Yes, thanks. Things don't seem to change much in your neck of the woods.'

'If only.'

Stephen found Melanie in a spacious and finely furnished office. Her clandestine job had clearly brought her promotion. She greeted him cheerfully and asked her personal assistant to bring in two cups of coffee. She looked him in the eye without saying anything and let him lead the conversation.

'I'm now an assistant military attaché in Warsaw, and I've flown over to—'

'Yes, I know all that.'

'Well, Melanie, I need your professional advice again.'

She looked at him enquiringly. Stephen launched into the long saga about Zofia Plucik and Anna Śnieżko, unburdening himself of a huge weight of guilt, bitterness and apprehension as he did so.

'What do I do now, Melanie? I'll have to come clean with MOD, won't I?'

She then took up the conversation, and what she went on to say astonished him.

'Neither of those women is any more your sister than I am. The young girl who brought you across to England in '43, and who was later to survive Auschwitz, was indeed Anna Śnieżko. Zofia Plucik, on the other hand, is well known to us as a Soviet sleeper agent. Assuming the identity of the dead Anna Śnieżko provided her with the perfect cover she needed to suborn or compromise a Polish-born attaché at the British Embassy. Or that's what her controllers will have thought.'

'But why target me? I'm hardly a high-flyer.'

'That may be so now, but you're already privy to all kinds of sensitive information, as well as being practised in covert intelligence-gathering. Your career profile points towards a position of considerable potential value to our Eastern Bloc friends. In any case, with your Polish-Jewish background you will have been marked out at an early age.'

Stephen remembered his brief encounter with that German diplomat after the school revue. But now he needed to know where Melanie Sledge fitted into this increasingly ominous picture.

'You've known about this Plucik woman all along, and yet you did not see fit to warn me about her. Why not?'

'Sometimes it's best to let these things run for a while. Anyway, we knew you could be trusted.'

'And what about the MOD?'

'We don't think they know anything about this.'

'Do you mean to tell me your outfit doesn't share this kind of information with the security people there?'

'Not automatically.'

Stephen was momentarily lost for words. Then he asked, 'Are you suggesting that I should not now report this can of worms to my bosses?'

'Yes, Stephen, I am. If they have any inkling of all this you're sure to know by the time you have finished being debriefed tomorrow, or whenever.'

Stephen finished his third cup of coffee and stood up to leave.

'Thanks, old friend. You really do understand what my career means to me, don't you?'

Melanie Sledge held out her hand to him and winked.

'Just say goodbye to your phoney sister, and carry on with your good work over there. By the way, I'm so glad for you that the MOD has shelved Op Minos.'

Stephen guessed what she meant and was impressed that she was au fait with the one operation that had been worrying him. His intelligence-acquisition training had not prepared him for intense doses of radiation.

XXXVI

Stephen's series of debriefings at the Ministry of Defence over the next two days were straightforward. He was pleased to be told that several of his more recent tour reports had been well received. He was complimented by several technical intelligence analysts on the quality of his photography. When the subject of Soviet nuclear weapons storage sites came up he took the opportunity to ask why Operation Minos had been so abruptly called off. He was half-expecting to be told simply that there was no further need for it. He was puzzled, therefore, when his question was met with silence. At no stage was he quizzed about social contacts with Polish nationals, so Melanie Sledge had probably been right after all.

When he arrived back in Warsaw he was feeling under the weather and was relieved to find no messages from Zofia Plucik, alias Anna Śnieżko. With a weekend to spare before re-embarking on tours of Soviet military restricted areas, he set out to relax with Erica. She also had time on her hands, and they spent an unbroken forty-eight hours together. In the alfresco privacy of the Saski Gardens she asked him whether he had finally broken off his dealings with his pseudo-sister. Without letting on about his dramatic discoveries since their last time together, he was able to reassure her, truthfully, that he had. In the less certain privacy of her flat, and her bed, they cheerfully traded intimacies which might titillate, but not inform, electronic eavesdroppers.

Come Monday, he was once again out in the bleak Polish countryside, having been tasked to pay a routine visit to the Commonwealth War Graves Commission Cemetery at Malbork. His methodical check for defaced or frost-damaged headstones set him oddly at ease, despite dormant anxieties and a cruel wind blowing in from the Baltic.

XXXVII

In the space of just two days Stephen's ordered and strictly accountable life was to be thrown into disarray. On his return to the embassy he found an MOD posting order awaiting him. His tour of duty as an attaché was to end, prematurely, in three months' time. His next appointment was to be that of a Grade 2 staff officer at Headquarters Salisbury Plain Training Area. He knew this to be a very small administrative office from which he would be working as little more than an overqualified range warden. To add insult to injury, the next OHMS envelope he opened contained a letter informing him that a number of high-level security clearances connected with his current job were revoked forthwith. No explanation was given.

Stephen suddenly understood how swiftly events had moved in his disfavour, and how there had almost certainly been an unforgivable betrayal of trust. His livelong Civil Service friend must surely have been working in cahoots with the security staff at the MOD. And when he was cold-shouldered several times in the corridors of the embassy he guessed that his amiable Jewish bedfellow had also been less than loyal to him.

Several long walks, alone, in the Saski Gardens served only to increase his dejection. He started to have more severe fits of dizziness, and scarcely felt well enough to attend a diplomatic drinks party laid on in the embassy canteen on the eve of his departure. The ambassador dropped in, but Erica Mendel was nowhere to be seen.

The next day Stephen set out at the crack of dawn in his overladen car. Driving along the potholed main road to the East German border, and soon afterwards down the Berlin corridor to Helmstedt, he ruefully flew past some of the railwatch hides from which he had recorded and photographed transiting Soviet hardware over the years. For him all this was now history, and yet history of which he was still a part. With no prospect of the Cold War ending there was a certain sense of reassurance that the world would continue to be a relatively safe place. Stephen had had first-hand experience of an East-West balance of supreme power and mutual deterrence which, for forty years, had made a full-scale nuclear war eminently improbable.

Once back in England, Stephen quickly set about rearranging both his professional and private life. A two-bedroom rented house in a small village on the west edge of Salisbury Plain materialised without delay. After a further week of disembarkation leave he reported to his new boss, an avuncular retired brigadier at HQ Salisbury Plain Training Area, who asked not a single question about his army career to date, let alone his recent work as an attaché. Stephen's awareness of being undervalued was not helped by the suspicion that so many years away from his parent regiment would deny him the inimitable support of the so-called regimental family.

With an English summer in the offing his spirits lifted a little as he set out on a series of Landrover trips across Salisbury Plain to familiarise himself with his huge area of responsibility. The mysterious archaeological sites, the fauna and flora of the untamed grassland, the treeless wind; all these simplified and refreshed him. And the constant rumbling of the guns on the Larkhill ranges made him feel secure. The proximity of close artillery support had always been reassuring to him as an infantryman, and even as an infant had he not been lulled to sleep by the blesséd sound of those guns?

Then one day he began to feel alarmingly unwell. As time went on his cocky lance-corporal driver ran out of jokes about hungover officers, and even began to express concern for him. Persistent nausea, and some sudden hair loss, eventually persuaded Stephen to undergo a medical examination. An army doctor referred him at once to a civilian specialist who promptly diagnosed radiation sickness.

Stephen had long been amused by the jocular expression "lose the will to live" when applied to nothing more than chronic boredom. But now it held quite a different meaning for him. He was feeling iller by the day. His treks over the plain were becoming increasingly irksome. In order to give himself brief respite from his wretched affliction he would take a daily newspaper with him. One day in June he parked up in a lay-by to work his way through the Queen's Birthday Honours. He was not surprised to find that two of his service colleagues had received awards in recognition of what he knew to be their work behind the Iron Curtain, and he felt ashamed to be deeply envious of public acknowledgment which he now knew would never come his way. His letter of congratulations to each of them would be going by second-class mail.

XXXVIII

By early September Stephen's radiation sickness, which had been ineffectively treated, was causing him to lose not only weight, but also hope. With seemingly no one to whom he could look for help or solace, his thoughts turned repeatedly to Anna Śnieżko. But his Christian upbringing had offered no promise of succour for the living by the dead.

The artillery impact areas at Larkhill are, paradoxically, a haven for wildlife. Even some rookeries there are known to be immune from the effects of high explosive.

Having carefully checked the published monthly forecast of live firing exercises, Stephen set out one Friday shortly before first light. After parking his car just inside a small wood he made his way on foot towards a spot marked on his training area map as Slay Barrow. The wind was getting up, and he could hear a halyard rattling insistently against a tall steel flagpole which he passed in the darkness. He could tell from that sound that a red flag was already flying. Twenty minutes later he reached the place, and settled down inside a clump of juniper by a heavily cratered earthwork.

As dawn began to break the whole area slowly came to life. First trilling birdsong, then a cacophony of noise from an alarmed pheasant. Through a sudden wave of nausea Stephen thought he heard the apocalyptic sound of hooves thundering by in the early morning gloom. As the sun rose above the only visible hill a hare loped past, and he could feel tiny insects crawling over his neck and face. He glanced at his watch, and was not taken by surprise when the first salvo of 155mm shells exploded just fifty yards from where he was sitting. He would have been profoundly deaf to the incoming second salvo which ended it all for him.

XXXIX

Major Stephen Yates' absence from work and the discovery of his abandoned car quickly led to a search of the Larkhill artillery impact area. The army board of enquiry which followed noted that a set of military ID discs had been found among the body parts, together with a shredded wallet containing a triple contact print of a registered child prisoner in Auschwitz. There had been no witnesses to what was deemed to be an unavoidable training accident.

It was not long before Miss Melanie Sledge had been identified as Stephen Yates' nominated next of kin. She had to take precious time off from important security work to wind up his slender estate, and to make arrangements for his unattended burial, close to the Polish war graves, in Tidworth Military Cemetery.

Acknowledgements

My wife Hazel and daughter Penelope, who both endured and enjoyed Cold War days with me behind the Iron Curtain, have played a key part in the writing of this book. Without Hazel's endless hours on her word processor and Penelope's literary guidance it would surely have never come to fruition.

I am greatly indebted to Helen Hart and Rowena Ball of SilverWood Books for placing me in the capable hands of Annie Broomfield. She patiently and cheerfully helped me to navigate my way through the labyrinth of contemporary publishing, sustaining my morale with sound suggestions and inspired ideas.

Lightning Source UK Ltd.
Milton Keynes UK
UKOW04f0015160817
307363UK00002B/322/P